Folktales from the Endless Frontier

Volume 1

Brett Lurie

Contents

Timeline of the Endless Frontier
All Titles Available Now!

04/19, 3766 *Sky Guard*

05/15, 3788 *The Rider in Black*

14/14, 3790 *The Case of the Gill Ripper*

07/22, 3799 *The Cold Brook Job*

09/17, 3799 *Of Duels and Debts*

11/01, 3800 *The Hunter and the Knight*

ACKNOWLEDGEMENTS

To Joanna Penn, Robert Enright, David B. Lyons, Ryan Cahill, Bethany Atazadeh, Petrik Leo, Mandi Lynn, Dale Roberts, Dave Chesson, MK Williams and the many others who provide indie authors with the tools, information and inspiration necessary to navigate the pages of publishing. These tales are dedicated to your wisdom and guidance.

DIVINITY
FROZEN FALLS
KARREDILE SOUND
GRAND SUMMIT
HAELOVAN FOREST
ANGELWOOD
GUARDIAN'S GLACIER
CRESCENT REALM
ELDER
THE RYTESIA SEA
GREY VALLEY
WILLOW WIND
HEAVEN SHADOW
THE SALT RAPIDS
WHITE STONE
SEA HAVEN
PINE FALL
BLACK STONE
CARMINE FRO
THE PILLARS O
THE IMPERIUM
HAVEN WHISPER
ARCHWO
EDGE CLIFF
DEADSET RIDGE
THE GORGE MAZE
MOSSWOOD PORT
BLACK LAKE
MOSSLAND SUMMITS
OX WELL
MIST
STORMGATE
VANDA
PRAIRIELAND
BLOOD BOULDER BASIN
RIDGESPIR
THE ELDRICH FOREST
THE TEMPLE OF JELLINOK
THE BLACK SAND HILLS
COPPER DESERT PASS
INDIGO COVE
PLATINUM HIL
BARREN ROCK
MIRAGE CANYON PASS
MIDWAY LAK
OLD SKULL VALLEY
RIVER POINT
DUNELAND
SOUTHERN FALLS
BENDING GROVE
SHELLBORN
DEAD MOON BAY
TO ROGUE HAVEN
COVE OF THE SOUTHERN SERPENT

Ice Wyrm Isle
Disciple's Rapture
Siren Song Isle
Watcher's Shore
Mount Morvius
Vellios Summit
Sanctuary
Raven Fort
The Holy Harbor
Peaks of Purification
Silverkeep
Lake Shal
Andro Coast
The High Imperium
Ash Valley
Eel's Mouth
Hollow Mesa
Cold Brook
Golden Creek
Onyx Canyon
Eastgate Harbor
Dreadbank
Crystal Flats
Vaeliz Estate
Cactustown
Vulture
The Valley of Tombs
Phantom Mesa
Draelekar

Sky Guard

I. First Mate

Sariya Vaeliz shivered as she floated across the sunken ship's darkened cabin. Her fingers slid over the wooden desk, the grandfather clock, the drifting glove. Nothing. There was nothing there. Sariya's body grew numb. The salty water passed through her mouth and out her gills. Her Vandeni ancestors had evolved to breathe underwater, and her Imperial ancestors had evolved to withstand the cold. Both halves of her genetics were displeased.

Her black hair danced in the current. Her toes curled into the wooden floor. Fragments of declining daylight reached through the shattered windows. Ondakkar tentacles wrapped around the ship. The deep groan of a sea serpent rose from the fathoms.

'Swallow your paranoia,' she told herself. 'The dark depths are having their way with your imagination. Those tentacles are but shifting shadows. That terrible groan was the creaking of the vessel.' But perhaps it *was* time to end this search.

How long had she rummaged through the sunken ship? An hour? Two? She had yet to find a glimmer of treasure, much less a chest of minted platinum. And while ondakkar had not been spotted near the surface for hundreds of years, eels and sharks would look to satisfy their hunger as darkness fell on the northern sea.

Sariya drifted over the top of the desk. 'Might as well search it while I'm in here,' she thought. Face-down and feet dangling toward the ceiling, she yanked the drawers open. The sliding hollow wood echoed through the water. Out flowed the contents of the desk: letter openers, utility tools, drawing devices... sewing kits? Why would a banker have a drawer full of threads and needles?

She spread her arms and swam under the desk. Her gaze fell on the floor, made of metal rather than wood. She ran her finger along the surface—there was a crease along the outside of the central panel. The amphibious girl almost choked on her excitement, and a mouthful of seawater. With a salty smile, she reached for the welder on her utility belt. The device sparked as it followed the crease, leaving a red-hot trail.

The hatch popped open with a low clank. Careful not to touch the scorching edges as she pulled the compartment open, Sariya was eager to feast her eyes on a mound of platinum.

Instead, a white robe covered her face. She shook her head and pulled the garment free, gliding back. A cluster of dresses, robes, hats and jackets floated up from the hatch, untwining as they hovered toward the ceiling. The clothing stretched and twirled in the current, as if donned by swimming spirits.

"No," Sariya whispered, hauling out the remaining clumps of cotton and silk. Nothing lay beneath the wardrobe. "No..."

Her teeth clenched with a muted rattle as her body floated upward. She *could* just stay underwater, and never have to face the embarrassment that awaited at the surface. The salt water would not only hide her tears—but embrace them.

The young girl sighed through her gills. She dragged her fingers down her face and glided upward. Swiping the drifting clothing out of her path, she swam through the cabin door, angling through the broken window. Another second in that sunken ship would drive her to madness.

Blue daylight rippled across the surface and beamed into the depths. Sariya allowed herself to ascend, minding the change in pressure. Her ears ached and popped as she surfaced. She welcomed a deep breath into her lungs, her preferred respiratory organs.

The day was younger than she had thought. Athenis' blue rays still pierced the height of the grey skies, though did little to warm the air.

"Well?" a voice shouted from behind. "What be down there, young Sariya?"

Her shivering neck tilted upward at the host of men and women crowding the *Ocean Flame*'s taffrail. Her jaw locked as she went to speak.

"It's... it's not a banking ship," she stuttered.

They leaned forward with a collective mix of whispers and gasps. Thraeliss of Morrigal stood with her scaled fingers interlocked, her hands shaking.

"It's a merchant ship," Sariya said with a sluggish wince. "Maybe a tailor's vessel. There was a vault made for a fancy wardrobe. But there's no platinum or gems to be had. Anything of value was likely removed before the vessel sank."

The crew's anticipation turned to a synchronized groan. "There may never have been nothin' of value at all," one of them shouted.

Thraeliss shook her head, her vertical pupils narrowing to thin slits, sharp as double-sided daggers. "The little princess has done it again."

Second Officer Halsik sat at the corner of the ship, frost in his black beard. "Are you really all that surprised?"

"It wasn't my fault!" Sariya's voice trembled as her palm slapped the water. "The chatter, the Imperial records. It all pointed toward a crashed banking vessel."

The crew laughed.

She shrank back, bobbling on the surface. How childish she must have sounded...

"Let's fire up the electro-sail, Captain," Halsik said. He spit overboard—in Sariya's direction. "This was a waste of time, like I warned ye."

"Yes!" Thraeliss shouted. "My blood may be cold, but so are my scales. And I don't reckon that to be natural." She earned a laugh from some of her crewmates.

The crew turned to Captain Bellacor. They cleared a path for his long stride. "Aye. Man your stations, lads," the captain instructed.

They hollered and cheered, breaking from the gathering. Captain Bellacor gave Sariya a lengthy sneer before turning away.

Eller was the only one who stayed behind. He tossed the flimsy tin ladder overboard with a nod and a heartening grin.

Sariya met his brown eyes and mouthed, "Thank you." The weight of her shame prevented the return of a smile.

Sariya grabbed the ladder. The glacial air bit her skin as she climbed. Her teeth rattled. Somehow, the water felt warmer. She fought an overwhelming urge to jump back in.

After climbing aboard, Eller handed her a thin towel. "Find anything nice to wear?" he asked with a smirk.

"I'm nowhere near the mood to make light of this, Eller," she said, drying her hair.

"Don't take it too hard, Sariya."

She looked down, shaking her head. "I can't believe I messed up again."

"You'll get it right next time."

"That's what you said last time."

Eller pulled his green jacket tight across his chest, covering every inch of his blue-grey skin. "Yeah, but I was just trying to make you feel better before." He gave her a soft punch in the shoulder. "I mean it this time."

Though she had no desire to smile, she could not help herself. "Encouraging as always."

He shrugged. "That's why I'm here."

"Sailor Vaeliz!" a gruff voice shouted from below. "Get yerself out of that swimwear and meet me in me cabin."

"Aye, Captain." She swallowed. "He does not sound happy," she said to Eller.

Eller pulled up his leather gloves by the wrist cuffs. "Oh, don't worry. Cap won't stay angry long. Especially not with you."

"I know he won't." Her eyes shifted to the crew, manning their duties on the lower deck. "That's why they hate me."

"They're just jealous," Eller said, his fingers tracing his goatee.

She shrugged and walked past him. "Not for any testament to me quality."

She stepped down the staircase to the main deck. The icy metal numbed her bare feet. Three Vandeni men and one Draekalagon woman scurried up the stairs. One of the men bumped Sariya's shoulder, and the collision was not accidental.

The ogling crew exchanged bitter whispers. She hid her eyes, pretending not to notice.

"Does the young lady of the palace wish for us to shuttle her anywhere else?" Dorgallik shouted over the hiss of his welder. The sparks reflected off his goggles, giving him the visage of a snarling dragon.

Thraeliss, brethren to Dorgallik through Clan Morrigal, handed him another tool. She covered her mouth with an exaggerated gasp. "Oh, how rude of me not to ask, Dorgallik." She curtsied. "Please let us know if there is anything we can do to serve you, m'lady."

Sariya scoffed and kept walking. Several crewmen laughed at the Draekalagons' jeering.

"Cut it out, the both of ye!" Halsik stood on the forward deck, hands in his belt. "She doesn't need to hear any of this right now." A grin slithered up his lips.

The deck fell quiet, save for the sizzling and banging of tools.

"At least have the decency to... draw the princess' bath and offer her a hot meal."

They hollered and laughed with him.

Halsik's belly rumbled with his merriment. "I'm sure she is just *famished* after her little swim."

Sariya bit her tongue until she reached the stairs leading to the subdeck. She turned around, unable to tame an eruption of rage. "Go to hell! All of ye."

Thraeliss and Dorgallik countered with deep bows. "Oh, Your Highness, please forgive us."

Halsik leaned over the deck. "When you decide you want to go back to your castle, let us know. We'll take you right in, won't we, mates?"

"Leave her be, lads!" Eller yelled from the stern of the ship.

Their ridicule and laughter carried onto the subdeck.

She could not look at herself in the mirror. But she forced herself. Just long enough to ensure that her vest was on straight, that her beige shirt was clean and that her belt was buckled over her loose slacks. She tied a grey bandana tight around her head, tucking her raven black hair away from her face. Her viridian-green eyes met their reflection and fell shut.

With a groan, she clasped the mirror's ornate, spiraling frame. She eyed the empty bed across from hers. 'Thank the Guardians that Mylia was not in here,' she thought. 'A minute to meself between mockeries is a humble request.'

Containers of makeup sat on the rosewood table to her right. She rested her long fingers on the eyeliner and lipstick, then shoved them away. Sariya Vaeliz managed to stomach a long look at her blue skin, at her angular face. Makeup—no makeup—they would belittle her regardless.

A roaring wave broke upon the circular window as Sariya exited the cabin. She marched through the dim amber lighting of the *Ocean Flame*'s halls, unbothered by the vessel's rocking. Making herself skinny, she slipped past a tall Imperial sailor gaiting down the opposite side of the corridor.

After climbing the stairs, she was back to the main deck. Several crew members stole a glance, then made damn sure not to look again.

They fell silent.

What were they talking about before she came up?

Sariya jumped back when two men stepped in front of her, holding a replacement chain for the electro-sail's mast. How could such a large vessel feel so small? "Please, excuse us," said one of the men: a mixblood, like Sariya.

She bowed her head with a slight smile.

Her breath shuddered. She shook a nervous tremble out of her gloved hands. A black door stood below the stern of the ship. Here, she halted, and her fingers clasped the bronze handle, shaped like a flaming skull. The door creaked open. She licked her chapped purple lips, stepped through and shut the door behind her. Standing tall, she locked her hands behind her back. "You asked for me, Captain?" A swallow slipped past the lump in her throat.

"At ease, Sariya." He tapped the screen on his desk, then his finger followed the blue glow of a digital map. A platinum skull, a long hourglass and a golden chalice sat atop his desk, swaying with the *Ocean Flame*. The model ships on his bookshelf tilted with the tides.

"A tailor's vessel?" His words were sharp on Sariya's ears. "If you were looking for work as a seamstress, I'm sure some of my garments could use mending."

Was he trying to comfort or deplore her? Probably both. "I'm sorry, Captain." She bit her lip, in search of speakable words. "I really thought I'd spotted us a plunder this time."

"Sariya," he said, looking up from his desk. "Not every piece of chatter that you pick up on your scanner is worth pursuit." He leaned back in his leather chair. "There be more to piracy than platinum and plunder."

"Aye, Cap." She slouched forward and nodded once. "But we haven't had us a rich find in some time. I know that you'd like to see a lift in profits. And that the lads and lasses could use a lift of spirit."

Bellacor twisted the silver ring on his finger. "Sariya, don't be worrying about such things. I have that handled."

"But I *want* to do more." She took a dragging step toward his desk. A flock of shadow gulls flew past the window behind him. "I want to be your best sailor, Captain."

"So that's what this is about." He crossed his hands over his stomach. "You're trying to secure the opening at third officer." He looked down and shook his head with a gruff chuckle. "Sariya, hoping to strike a rich find with nothin' to go off but eavesdropping and old Imperial records is no way to win them over."

She crossed her arms and shifted her weight. "What does it matter? They hate me anyway."

The captain raised his hands. "They don't hate you—"

"Besides," Sariya snapped, interrupting. "I'm not after third mate. I want first."

The captain's green eyes widened, sparkling in the shadow of his black tricorn hat. "First officer?"

And just like that, Sariya had tipped her hand. "Yes," she said with a sigh. "I am more qualified than anyone aboard."

"I don't know about that—"

"It's true and you know it." She rested her palms on his glossy ebony desk. "I've proven time and time again that I am capable of manning any station on the *Ocean Flame*. Yet its crew still treats me like I'm some spoiled little Imperial noble who is only here because you allow me to be."

"They're just giving ye your due heckling, Sariya. They do it to everyone."

Her voice rose. "No. They don't."

The captain removed his hat and pushed his black hair away from his face with a sharp sigh. "Look, I am still going to put you forward for third mate. Halsik was Jaggenskelt's first choice to succeed him when he stepped down. I can't go against his wishes. Halsik is the current second officer. The crew would question my judgment if I passed him up for first."

"Halsik. Great." She stomped a boot on the wooden floor. "Have fun with that belly of joy."

"Surround yourself with those whom you may not see eye to eye with." He leaned forward, pointing at her. "It forces ye to understand perspectives that would normally pass ye by."

She let go of a trembling sigh and nodded.

"Also," the captain said with a shrug. "Have you thought about what your appointment to first officer would mean for Eller? Not only is he popular with the crew, he's also been one of my most loyal sailors." Captain Bellacor grabbed a crystalline glass on his desk and poured a splash of whisky from the nearby bottle. "Would you want to tell him that he's not getting the promotion to second officer? Because ye snaked yourself into first?"

"Are you kidding?" Sariya reached for the captain's glass. "I'd be charmed to see the look on his face."

"Sariya." He frowned. "Just mind yer duties. Work with diligence and yer head held high. And I promise, I'll still put you down as my nomination for third officer."

Sariya's blue face scrunched as she took a sip of the whisky. "Even with your endorsement, they'll turn me down." She slapped the glass back on his desk. "Their love for you is clearly rivaled by their distaste for me."

"I'll veto their vote if I'm unhappy with the result."

"No, Father!" Sariya stood wide, fists clenched. "I don't want ye to appoint me for third. I want first. And I'll earn it."

"No!" The captain stood, and his chair rolled back.

Sariya shrank and recoiled. She was taller than him. But when his voice thundered across his cabin and his stance straightened, Captain Bellacor was a mountain.

"You *will* earn your way into rank on this vessel, Sariya—not by seeking remote sunken treasures or undercutting fellow crewmen. You'll earn your way up the way that Halsik did, the way that Eller did..." His stare was dour and penetrating. "The way that *I* did."

She looked down, hiding her eyes. "I understand."

He sidestepped the desk and rested his hand on her wrist. "No more escapades. I can't be having ye wasting any more of the ship's time or resources. We make for Rogue Haven to resupply." His hand clutched her shoulder. "Now get yerself to the top of the lookout tower. There's a storm coming. We'll need your eyes up there in case our navigation instruments run three sheets to the wind."

"Aye, Cap," she said with a slight nod.

"Alright. You're dismissed, sailor."

II. The Tower

A wide grin climbed up Sariya's face when she exited the captain's quarters. She found many duties on the *Ocean Flame* grueling. Washing the deck was torture. Cleaning the crew quarters was boring. Working the mess hall was unappetizing. In contrast, working in navigation, telecommunication and artillery management *was* stimulating. But Sariya's favorite station was the lookout tower. The high climb gave her a rush of adrenaline. Once atop it, she could scan the satellites for unencrypted chatter. And no one could stop her. 'Father didn't say anything about listening,' she thought as the flimsy metal ladder stirred in the wind. Best of all, the lookout tower offered complete solitude.

She climbed over the railing, her boots clacking on the metal platform. The icy air soothed her spirits. Grey clouds swirled overhead. The blue-green ocean grew darker by the mile as they sailed away from the Northern Sea. She pulled her blue jacket tight across her breast and closed every button before wrapping her cloak around her neck. The last rays of Athenis' blue light of life were receding.

'Only going to get colder. Toughen up and get used to it.'

After looking through her spyglass for several minutes, Sariya took a seat on the platform. She attached an auditory data system to her right ear. After she did some tuning and heard only static, she let her frown give way to a smirk. She had locked onto a conversation passing through the satellites in Eramaa's planetary orbit.

"I ordered this wine over a month ago. Where is it?"

A sharp voice replied, *"Sir, our records indicate that there was a delay with the merchant. You need to contact them."*

"If it's in your records, why hadn't you informed me? I have customers—"

'Boring,' Sariya thought, adjusting the frequency.

"You know how much I miss you. They've kept me in this damn mine too long. But our relief team should be coming in the next few days."

"Good. I can't bear the thought of sleeping alone for another week."

"And that is quite a private call," Sariya whispered to herself, adjusting the frequency again. "They really ought to encrypt that." Her eyes caught a sizable splash in the distance. She stood and looked through her golden spyglass. A white smoke whale rode the waves on the ocean surface. Its glossy skin was bathed in the dusk of the sapphire-and-amethyst sky.

Sariya smiled and lit a cigarillo. Another conversation began. *"I told you that you have to lock up the barrels before..."*

'No,' Sariya thought. She turned toward the ship's front. Still no storm in sight.

"The tides are looking rather wild out there tonight, aren't they...?"

'No.'

"The lighthouse doesn't seem..."

'No.'

"Someone please bring me my..."

'No.'

She reached for the off button of her device. But a new frequency piqued her interest.

"Yeah, my team finished repairs this afternoon. She should be ready to set sail again."

"And is Madame Denavoss already taking flight?"

Sariya gasped, covering her other ear to better hear the woman's reply.

"Sometime in the next day or two. Katrielle is overly eager to get this flying tank off the ground."

"Sea Haven doesn't suit her fancy?"

"I don't think it suits her suspicion. She has two guards at the vessel's entrance at all times. And you should see how she has this ship outfitted. Enough artillery to hold off a Draelek fleet. And to think that the good madame uses it as a floating ballroom..."

Sariya stomped out her cigarillo, then leapt over the railing and climbed down the ladder, paying more mind to her speed than her safety. Hyperventilation accentuated the sharp pain in her chest and the dry ache of her throat.

She leapt to the deck. The crew turned at the sound of her landing. Halsik stood near. He displayed a data system to a group of sailors, giving orders and offering instruction.

"Look," he said with a slight smirk. "The castle rat has climbed down from her ivory tower. Is she done playing pirate for the day?"

Sariya turned from Halsik and his snickering underlings. She looked over her shoulder at his bulging belly. "Are ye done eating all the rations?"

The sailors' mockery turned to the second mate. Sariya held her chin high as she sauntered away, flaunting a wide grin.

She pushed the doors to the captain's quarters open. "Captain," she called out. His office was empty. His chair was pulled out. The digital screen on his desk was on.

"Captain," she said, stepping toward the rows of rectangular windows at the back of the cabin. She pushed open the door between the two sets of windows. As she suspected, Captain Bellacor stood at the balcony, leaning over the railing.

"Look, Sariya." He did not turn to face her. "The cetaceans are riding the *Ocean Flame*'s wake."

She stepped beside her father and watched the barreling cetaceans, squeaking and purging seawater through their blowholes. "They're always glad to ride our wake."

"Do you remember how excited you'd be to see them when you were a little lass?" He took a drag from his cigar, meeting Sariya with a soft smile. "You'd make me wake ye up in the middle of the night anytime a whale or dolphin poked its head out."

Sariya smiled back, then looked out to sea. "Father, I have to tell you something."

"What are you doing down here, Sariya?" His hand rested on the bronze hilt of his rapier. "You're supposed to be up in the tower. If ye needed to talk to me, I *know* you have yer data system up there. Just send a transmission."

"I know. But I had to tell ye this face-to-face." She stepped closer. "It's about the *Sky Guard*."

The captain's thick brow furrowed. "What about it?"

"It's undergone repairs at Sea Haven. It will be unmanned and lightly guarded for the next few nights." She flashed a smirk. "Just enough time for us to commandeer her."

He sighed and shook his head. "You've been listening to satellite chatter again."

"Yes, but—"

"Sariya, what did I just tell you?"

"I know. But it's the *Sky Guard*! And it's docked in Sea Haven. We know those docks better than anyone, Cap." She reached forward and grasped the top of her father's hand. "Your ship, Father. The ship that *you* designed is sitting there for us to take. We need a second ship. The *Ocean*

Flame will always be home, but she's too small for your ever-growing crew. And while she may be swift, she can't fend off a fleet on her own. You have made some enemies at sea, Cap. You should hear the other captains speak of ye over the satellite network." The ocean sang with the wind, and the spray of the waves tickled her face. "I know you've wanted to find another ship for us. Why not *your* ship?"

Captain Bellacor pulled his hand from Sariya's grip. "Did they mention the *Sky Guard* by name?"

Sariya's lips pursed. "What do you mean?"

"In the conversation that you intercepted, Sariya." He turned to face her, taking that imposing shape of a mountain. "Did they refer to the vessel by name?"

She looked down and shook her head. "No."

"So, for all we know, it's some useless cargo barge."

She reached toward him. "Father, no. The vessel they described was—"

"We're not risking the lives of the crew to ransack Sea Haven for what could be another dead lead." The captain crossed his arms behind his back, displaying his maroon jacket and bronze belt buckle.

"But Father." Her fists clenched. "I am *sure* this time."

"You were sure every time before this." He turned away, leaning over the deck again. "Get back to the tower, Sariya. Stormy skies are shifting along our course." He kept his daughter in the corners of his eyes. "We can find a hefty contract in Rogue Haven. And after we retain some earnings, perhaps we can look at investing in a second vessel."

She crossed her arms. "And it'll be mossy rot compared to the *Sky Guard*."

"Sailor Vaeliz." His frigid enunciation shook the cigar clenched between his teeth. "Get yerself back to that lookout tower, or I'll have ye on barracks duty for the week. We clear, lass?"

Sariya bowed her head and shut her eyes for a long blink. "Aye, Captain Vaeliz." She stamped off the balcony and out of his quarters.

III. Shield of the Storm

Flashing bursts of lightning revealed hungry black clouds. "Storm-front, ten miles!" Sariya yelled from the top of the lookout tower.

"Aye!" Eller replied from the stern, one hand on the *Ocean Flame*'s helm. "Adjusting course and reducing speed."

"Copy that, mate!"

Purple voltage surrounded the electro-sail, propelling the ship. The mechanical lightning shrank, hushing the *Ocean Flame*'s roar. Thunder growled in the black clouds; the wild lightning's fury refused to cease.

"Avast!" Halsik hollered from the front of the ship. "Raise that storm shield before a drop of rain touches the bowsprit. Don't linger a minute, ye lazy urchins. All hands to your stations! Batten down the hatches! All hands on!"

The storm shield was her father's design. It was a clear material that angled upward from the inside of the hull to mitigate the damages of rain, wind and lightning. The curved screen also kept the sailors on deck from tumbling overboard. Unfortunately, the storm shield did not reach the top of the lookout tower.

The ship swerved from side to side, surrounded by echoes of thunder. Sariya wiped her optical system with her cloak and magnified her spyglass.

She looked north. No oncoming whales or sea serpents.

She looked south. No nautical lights. No signs of other vessels along their course.

She looked east. No whirling ripples of maelstroms.

She looked west. No rogue waves threatened to damage the *Ocean Flame*'s broadside.

Droplets of rain sprinkled the roots of her hair. She pressed an icon on her communication device. "Hey, navigation chaps. How be yer readings down in the dark, dainty, *safe* clutches of the subdeck?"

"Functional," Ithia's voice crackled in her ear. "Not picking up any foreign objects. But the storm is confusing our weather sensors. We're having trouble tracking the epicenter."

"Copy that, lass," Sariya said, leaning over the railing. "I'll keep an eye on the summit."

"Stay sharp, lil' lassie."

Sariya leaned over the railing, looking portside. She turned on the infrared setting of her optical system. Looking through her spyglass, she surveyed the black sea for possible courses. She gasped—an area in the distance looked to be devoid of clouds.

"Eller!" she shouted toward the ship's stern.

"Aye?" he replied.

"Adjust our course, thirty degrees port!"

She could hardly hear his reply under the surrounding roll of thunder. "You sure? Haven't heard anything about that from nav." The scattering raindrops escalated to a steady downpour.

"Aye, I'm sure. And no, ye wouldn't." She pointed toward their current course. "The storm is grogging their weather scanners. But the clouds be thinner five miles southeast."

Eller hesitated. "How do you know that's not the storm's eye?"

"I don't claim to!" Sariya said with a boisterous giggle. "If it is, then you better be ready to handle that helm better than you handle your liquor!"

"Don't look at me!" Eller replied. "If you sail us into the heart of the storm, it's you who'll be sailing us out."

"It'd be an honor, mate!" She faced forward, holding the railing with both hands. A bolt of lightning struck the front electro-sail, giving the *Ocean Flame* a short burst of speed. 'Sometimes the only way through the storm,' she thought, 'is to sail through its heart.' She felt the cool rain trickle down her neck. 'Even if you have to set sail on your own.'

After they adjusted the *Ocean Flame*'s course, the vengeance of the sea subsided. Choppy waves and a light drizzle still salted the mood, but the storm no longer presented a threat. Or any fun.

Hours had passed when Sariya heard the nasally snarl of an Imperial accent. "Madame Sariya," the prim voice of Eldofain said from the ladder. His words rolled off his tongue. "I have come to spell you of your lowly duties. You may return to your regal Imperial quarters now."

Sariya grunted and leaned over the railing. "Don't call me *madame*. I sleep in the same quarters as you, Eldofain." He set foot on the tower. Her green eyes narrowed like a predator on prey. Water trailed down her forehead. "Are you not from the Imperium as well, you cretinous keel feeder?"

He leaned forward, hovering over her face. "*I* am Imperial. *You* are a mixblood parasite who doesn't know her place."

"Well, I certainly know yours." She shoved him away and leapt onto the ladder. "When Rytekos strikes you with a bolt of lightning, I'll utilize your corpse as shark bait." She gave an open-finger salute before sliding down the ladder.

Nightfall deepened. Sariya lay in bed on her back, both eyes open. She peered at Mylia, out cold and snoring. On any other night, this would be irritating. But on this night, Sariya was grateful that Mylia's respiratory ailments would keep her awake.

After midnight, when the ship fell quiet, she checked the *Ocean Flame*'s coordinates on her data system. It was in position. It was time. She grabbed her bandana, a fresh set of clothing, a short rapier and her favorite pistol, then tiptoed out of the cabin.

Sariya Vaeliz entered the control room. Only two sailors were on duty, and they were in no mood to question her presence. On the control panel behind them, she pressed the icon marked "Ancillary Craft," and touched a second icon marked "Dispatch."

A light drizzle sprayed the upper deck. Few crew members were present, and most of them were preoccupied. She leaned over the taffrail. There it was. The small ancillary clipper drifted along, locked to the ship's keel. 'Thank the Guardians. No one heard the gears moving over the growl of the electro-sail and the roar of the storm.' Sariya smiled and pulled out a rope from her pack, unwinding its tight bundle.

"What are you doing?" a voice called from behind.

Sariya spun around. Eller approached. She pressed her finger to her lips. "Shhh!" She looked over his shoulder, making sure he had not alerted anyone. "Don't worry about it, Eller. Just get back to work."

"I'm off duty," he said with a tight squint. "And... I reckon that you are too."

"Aye." Sariya bit her lip and nodded.

"So..." He leaned over the ship's forepeak and muttered, "What are you doing with the attack boat?"

"I'm going after the *Sky Guard*," she said, tying a tight knot around the railing.

"Oh, come on, Sariya. You can't do that." His blue-grey face blocked her view of the small craft. "Your father outright rejected that idea. He told me himself."

"I know he did," Sariya said, pushing his face away. "He said I was endangering the crew and the integrity of his vessel. So, I am not taking his crew—nor his vessel. Just me humble self."

"Sariya, come on—"

"Don't try and stop me," she said, wagging her finger. "The decision has been made." She spoke through a wide smile. "And if ye try callin' for help, I'll put a sleeper bolt in ye." She tapped the curved handle of her pistol and tossed a satchel of supplies into the boat below. "We clear on that, matey?"

"Yeah, clear. But you can't do this, Sariya." He scratched the back of his head. "Your father would kill me if he found out that I let you go."

Sariya Vaeliz chuckled and hopped over the taffrail, sliding along the rope and into the small boat. "Then don't let me go," she said with a sharp whisper, her gemlike eyes glimmering upon him.

He leaned down, brow furrowed and twitching. "I don't follow."

"Come with me."

Eller looked skyward. "You've got to be kidding me."

"Seems to me that it's your only option. You couldn't stop me, so you had to come with me. My father would *surely* understand that." She shrugged. "Besides, it'll be an adventure!"

The third mate's body drooped low. He groaned and whispered to himself. After leaping overboard, he slid down the rope and into the small boat.

"That's the spirit," she said, firing up the electro-motor.

He ogled her. "This better not cost me my job."

"It won't."

Eller cut the rope tying the attack boat to the *Ocean Flame*. Sariya disengaged the locks from its hull and disembarked. "Hey matey," she said, leaning toward Eller. "Thanks for coming along."

Eller sighed, watching the *Ocean Flame* as they left its shadow. His glare tightened and shifted to Sariya. "Did you plan this somehow? Dragging me along?"

Her eyebrows rose. "Maybe."

IV. Chain of Commandeer

The boat sped across open water, riding rough swells. After several hours, the drizzle ceased, and the black clouds dissipated. Sapphire-and-amethyst skies peaked above the fog. The silver light of the twin moons offered a sparkling kiss to the ocean's purple surface.

Sariya and Eller took shifts piloting the boat. When one pirate took the helm, the other rested. The ancillary craft was swift and maneuverable, suited for skirmishes or for use as an emergency lifeboat, though it was not meant for long trips. With luck, the craft would take them as far as they needed: to the Imperial shore.

'If it breaks down, Eller may just push me overboard.'

Athenis rose. Its blue light brushed Sariya's face, and her eyes opened.

"Oh good, you're awake," Eller said with a quick nod. "It's your turn at the helm."

Sariya groaned. "How's our course looking, mate?"

"We're making good time." Eller leaned back, one hand on the wheel. The motor roared behind him, leaving a thin trail of electric beams. "We should be there later this afternoon if we keep this pace." Soft winds blew through his thick brown hair. Athenis painted a dim aura around his blue-grey skin.

Sariya stood and stretched her arms. She slid her long black gloves over her hands. Their silver embroidery glittered in the sea's purple reflection. She took a sip of water and let out a yawn before moving to the back of the boat. "I'm ready when you are," she said, crossing her legs and leaning toward Eller.

"You sure you don't want to wake up a bit first?" he asked. "Would be a shame if you crashed us into a lighthouse before we could even attempt this silly little plan of yours."

"I'm okay. I'm sure ye'd fancy a break," she said, lips pursed to the side. "Kind of ye to consider me, though."

He slowed the boat and buttoned his red vest. Wobbling to his feet, Eller stepped to the boat's front. Sariya took hold of the helm. She giggled when he unbuttoned his vest again before lying down. He leaned back on his elbows, taking down a gulp of water. "Remind me, Sariya Vaeliz. Why am I here again?"

Sariya tendered a warm smile. "Because I'm your dear friend and your favorite sister of the sea." She flashed a wink. "Also, ye didn't want to deal with me father's retribution."

He snapped a finger. "Oh right. That." He slouched back, a sour curl on his lips. "An Imperial jail cell pales in comparison to whatever your father would have in store for me if I let you go alone."

Sariya chuckled. A refreshing mist brushed her face as the boat climbed a steep wave. "We're not going to jail, Eller. I know it for certain."

His eyes rolled. "And *what* could make you so certain?"

"You, sailor," she said with a slight smirk. "You said I would get it right this time."

Eller shut his eyes, covering his face with his black leather jacket. "Of course. *This* is what I get for encouraging you."

After several hours, they crossed into Imperial waters. The deep purple of the sea brightened. In the distance, the shore of Sea Haven came into view. A long harbor stretched from white shores, enclosed on each side by rock walls. Above the harbor stood a small town, built along a rocky hill; and looming over the town was Sea Haven Castle. Its towers pierced the shining violet sky, extending past the jagged cliffs and frosted trees. A white road extended from the castle and around the summit, all the way down to the harbor.

"Damn," Sariya said, slowing the craft.

"What is it?" Eller shaded his eyes with his hand, looking toward Sea Haven.

"The airship isn't at the harbor. That means…" She pointed skyward. "Katrielle has it docked at the castle." A vessel rested dormant in the sky, casting shadow on the towers.

Eller took a sip of water. "How do we get to it, then?"

"There's a secret entrance in the back. We can access it using the path along the cliffs," Sariya said. "Centuries ago, it was used to sneak in nightly companions for an elder lord."

He turned to her with a curious gaze. "How do you know that?"

"I was raised at Sea Haven Castle."

"Sure." His head tilted. "But you seem to know quite a bit about this secret entrance."

"Because I used to use it to sneak out, matey."

"Why'd you leave, anyway?"

"Sea Haven?"

"Yeah. Castle life. Servants, ballrooms, hors d'oeuvres. Seems to me like you had it made."

Sariya looked to the crests of the waves. "One would think so from the outside. So would I if I were you. But to me, noble life was hell."

"Sorry, I didn't mean—"

"No, it's okay, El." She offered him a reassuring smile. "It's just… when I saw me mother and me cousin, I did not see happy people. I did not see a fulfilling future. Sure, they have a host of servants. They have fancy dresses. They have friends in high places. But they viewed the world with nothin' but cold resentment. A need to keep up appearances filled them with a toxic, repressed anger. That anger followed their every step, every decision. My mother had to make sure that her castle had the highest tower on the western shore. Katrielle, my cousin, had to display the rarest gem with the finest cut at the ball on Cleric's Day."

Sariya looked down and shook her head. Eller encouraged her with a warm expression.

"They had so much, yet nothing fulfilled them. With every ballroom dance class, every lesson on courtly etiquette, every snobbish noble who wanted to arrange a betrothal before I was even of age, I saw a life laid in misery. Fancy misery, but misery nonetheless."

Eller laughed.

"When me father offered another path, I did not hesitate. With me father, on the sea, I was happy. I did not care if I would ever be rich again. Hell, I could be poor forever. But at least me life is me own."

"Well, I'm sure happy to share the sea with you, Sariya Vaeliz. Pain in the neck though you may be."

"Likewise, El."

She slowed the thrusters to a wakeless speed as they entered the harbor. Large cargo barges and small attack cruisers drifted in even rows, anchored along the titanium docks.

"When was the last time that you were here?" Eller asked.

"Four years ago."

"Wow. Haven't visited once?"

"No," she replied. "It's not as if they'd be keen on receiving me."

An aroma of moss and fish invaded the air. Sariya hopped off the boat. She stumbled as she set foot on the dock. The stability of land was a strange sensation for her knees. Eller handed her a chain, and she locked the boat to the docking station.

An elderly man approached, stomping down the harbor. "Hold!" he said, raising his hand.

"Let me do the talking," Sariya said.

The man's torso hunched over his tall Imperial frame. His wrinkled grey skin wobbled with his steps. "It's four platinum per night to station a boat to dock five."

Sariya placed her hands on her hips and presented the man with a bright smile. "That won't be an issue, kind sir."

"Yes, yes." He scrolled through his mobile data system. "How many nights do you plan on staying?"

"Just one," Sariya replied.

"And what is your business in Sea Haven?"

"We're merchants from down in Vanda." Sariya looked toward the village. "We were eager to explore some fine Imperial markets. We aim to resell some of your local products to untraveled Vandeni."

"I see, I see." The old man's green dress jacket fluttered in the wind, revealing his tight stockings and pointy leather shoes. "Your watercraft," he said, smacking his chapped grey lips. "This appears to be an ancillary boat from a larger vessel." His grim eyes narrowed on Sariya. "You didn't steal it, did you?" He looked to Eller, then back to Sariya.

"Of course we did!" was her instinctive reply. She felt Eller gawking at her with nervous confusion. "But we stole it from pirates. The crime cancels itself out."

The old man held his breath. His grey skin tightened around his nose. After a moment, he burst into laughter. Sariya followed suit, and Eller joined.

"That's a good one," he said. "Please, sign here."

He handed Sariya the data system. She signed a fake name and passed the device back. Paying through a digital transfer would leave a trail to her account. So, she placed four platinum coins into his hand.

"Say," he said with a smile. "You wouldn't by any chance be part Imperial, would you, miss?"

"I am," Sariya said with a nod. "On me mother's side. Me father is from Rogue Haven."

"Well, that sure explains the accent and blue skin," he said with a dry laugh. "But you are quite tall for a Vandeni woman. Gave you right away."

"Why thank you!" Sariya said. 'I think,' she thought.

"You two have a pleasant evening," he said with a tip of his wide tricorn hat. "May the Guardians bless your stay."

"Thank you for your service," Sariya said with a slight bow.

Her breath turned to steam when it touched the air. She had forgotten just how damn cold the High Imperium was. The ice caps were a different type of cold—a cold so bitter that it numbed the senses. But the Imperial cold stabbed you to the marrow like a bloodthirsty icicle. A thicker jacket would have been a wise choice.

The dock led to a small dirt road, topped with a thin sheet of snow, wood chips and fallen needles from the surrounding purple pines. Their footsteps crunched the snow and dead leaves. Sariya slipped but caught her balance when the trail turned uphill.

"Ya alright there, mate?" Eller said, reaching for her wrist.

She nodded and raised her hand. "Aye. Just gettin' me land legs back under me."

The dirt path wound to a road of grey-white stone. A wall of the same stone wrapped around the base of the hill. The pirates stepped through the gate to the other side of the wall. Gossiping voices with Imperial accents resounded through the streets. The mossy smell of fish from the dock faded, replaced by the sizzle of seared gold tail and crispy smoke from the tavern grill. Traffic congested the road. Men and women strode about with cloaks flowing behind or fur coats wrapped tightly around their bodies.

A church of the Order of the Guardians captured their gaze. Its tall silver tower shone in the blue daylight. Its blue, green and red stained-glass windows depicted sacred stories of the Guardians and the houses of old.

A deep roar interrupted their viewing. The pirates sprang back. A snow tiger stood before their path. Its fangs were sharp enough to tear through metal, and its jaws could devour Sariya's head in one bite.

"Whoa, whoa," the rider said, pulling the tiger's reins back. "Easy there, girl. Easy."

The tiger stepped back, its paws leaving wet prints on the street.

"Please forgive us," the rider said with a limp wave. "She was just trying to steer you from her path. She's perfectly harmless."

"Yeah, she seems... very friendly," Eller said, adjusting the red collar of his shirt.

Sariya waved back at the rider. "It's quite alright, sir. We shoulda had the mind to pay more attention to our steps."

"Your accent," the rider said, a curious smile on his grey lips. "Are you an Islander or an Imperial?"

She let out a short sigh. "Both," she said with a nod. "My father's an Islander. My mother is from the Imperium."

"Ah, how exotic." He pulled down his brown hood. "I could not quite place your dialect. Islander pronunciation. But you still have some Imperial inflection in there."

Sariya's lips pressed together. "Good to know."

The man patted the white head of his snow tiger. "We best be off. Apologies once again. Guardians' grace be with you."

"And with you," Sariya said with a bow of her head. She leaned over Eller's shoulder and whispered, "I swear. If one more person mentions my accent..."

"Yes, I hate it too." He crossed his arms and looked her way. "Sariya, is there a back way to this secret entrance? Not that I dislike absorbing the culture, but our blue skin and amphibious tendencies make us stick out like spearheaded sharks in shallow water."

"Maybe you should do the talking," Sariya said with a cackle. "You aren't quite as blue as I."

"True. But I'm also not as well versed in Imperial conversational customs."

Sariya brushed her hair behind her ear. "We can take the back alleys. Last thing we need is for the 'two oddly dressed Vandeni folk who just sailed in' to become the talk of the town."

She led him between two short buildings. Glass tubes ran overhead, sheltering beams of electricity. The two large cylinders stretched to smaller tubes in the alley, feeding power into the surrounding buildings.

Icicles stemmed from the power transfer cylinders. Mounds of snow were dirtied by boot prints, as well as the tracks of snow tigers and titan wolves. Workers gathered in the alleys for breaks. A barkeep stepped out of the back door of his tavern for a replacement barrel of ale. But the alley had few other dwellers or passersby.

She led Eller up a windy side street. Fancy buildings stood by the road, topped with narrow towers and fine-cut layers of spiraling brick—as if each structure was a small castle.

At the top of the circling road was a rock cliff. Sariya climbed the rocks, and Eller followed behind. "Watch your step here," she said as she shimmied along the edge. "It's quite a drop."

"What are you talking about?" Eller's eyes fell to the ground. "The drop down can't be more than... holy hell!"

As Sariya rounded the curve, the cliffside declined at a steep, aggressive angle. Jagged rocks awaited along the slope, accompanied by the furious crash of violet waves.

"Sariya." Eller's breath shook. "This may be your worst escapade yet."

She turned with a cackle. "Oh Eller, you'll be fine. It ain't no different than climbing up to the crow's nest." Her hand dragged along the wall. "Besides, if I could do it when I was thirteen, you can do it now." She leaned over the cliff. "Though I do remember this pathway being wider when I was a lil' lass. Doesn't look like they've kept up the maintenance."

"No, no." Eller hugged the wall, sidestepping toward her. "I do not want to hear that right now, my friend."

"Don't worry," Sariya said, walking backward. "We'll sing to keep our spirits high."

"Please don't."

She sang, *"I hear the fair maiden's call on the distant Island shore."*

"Sariya, stop."

"The lads and lasses beg of me: bring her on aboard."

"How are you walking backwards? Watch where you're going!"

She stretched her hand to the sky and belted another line. *"But I can't ye see, as they ask of me. Me mates don't know I'm torn."*

"By the life light of Athenis, please don't let her fall." He clasped his hands together, as if in prayer.

"Though my heart does fall with the maiden's call, it's the sea which I love more."

They made their way along the cliffside. Shadow gulls squawked at one another, circling the shore and diving for fish. "Hold tight, Eller," Sariya said.

"Not much to hold on to." He cleared his throat. "But I take your meaning."

She grinned. After ducking below a protruding boulder, they came upon a flat stone, large enough for the pirates to stand on without fearing for their safety. Against the cliff rose a wooden door sealed by a metal frame.

"This is it." Sariya removed a clip from her utility belt and knelt on one knee. "Oh no."

"What is it?" Eller asked, stepping forward.

"They've replaced the keyhole with an electric lock." She pointed to the spiraling door handle, mauled by the brass faces of miniature tigers on the top and bottom. "I can't pick an electric lock."

"The door's made of wood." He pressed his palm on the doorframe. "Can't we just break it down?"

Sariya shook her head. "The *outer casing* is made of wood. But it's covering solid steel."

Eller's hand fell under his chin. The rings on his fingers stroked his goatee. "Are you absolutely sure that this is the same exact door that you used to sneak out of?"

She took a long look at the chips, lines and grooves of the wooden panels. "Positive."

"Stand back," he said, reaching into his jacket pocket for his utility tool.

She squinted. "Are you going to hack the mechanism?"

Eller raised an eyebrow. "In a sense." He activated the welder setting on his tool. Sparks flew as blue flame touched the digital panel on the old entrance. After a moment, something in the door clicked. With a dead echo, the wooden door budged free from the metal frame and cracked open.

"How'd you know that would work?" Sariya asked.

"You said it was the same old door that was always there." Eller put his utility tool away and pulled on his lapels. "I knew that meant that there was no emergency auto-latch. Just an old door with an electric lock."

"Clever, matey," Sariya said with a smirk. "But we gotta get a move on. Just because they didn't install an auto-latch doesn't mean that they didn't install an alarm." She pushed the door open and entered Sea Haven Castle.

Dust flooded her nostrils. Darkness swallowed her steps. "Where'd that damn thing go?" She reached high, walking along the left side. "There it is." A long chain dangled from the ceiling. With a firm pull, the chain clacked and rattled. Yellow lights flickered overhead, giving view to columns of octagonal pillars. The tops of the pillars curved across the ceiling, connecting with one another in a series of archways.

"Let's move," Eller whispered.

Rows of barrels and metal crates sat stacked on each side of the walkway. Eller and Sariya's footsteps rang with a cold reverberation against the stone floor.

"You've got to admire Denavoss values." Her deep breath caught the scent of the oak barrels. "More wine than siege rations in their undercroft. By the moons, am I glad that—"

"Keep your voice down." Eller's stern glare flashed in the yellow light. "Tell me about it later. We gotta stay sharp."

Sariya nodded. "Aye."

They treaded with care across the cellar. At the opposite end of the room, Sariya spotted the stone stairs along the wall. She pointed toward the stairwell. Eller looked ahead and signaled for her to go first. They crept forward, moving through the shadows.

Voices resonated through the hall. Sariya and Eller dispersed, ducking behind separate pillars. She clutched the handle of her pistol as the voices grew nearer. Her breath stopped.

But the voices passed by in the upper confines of the castle. The pirates remained undiscovered. They let out a deep sigh and approached the staircase.

Dust wafted from under their boots with each step up. At the top stair, Sariya placed her ear to the wooden door. She flashed Eller a thumbs-up. Despite her giving the door only a delicate push, it creaked with the wrath of a dying breath. Sariya winced at the sound and peeked her head into the hall—the coast was clear.

Thick warmth surrounded her body. In an instant, she felt over-dressed. The chandelier bled cold blue from spiraling crystals. With a cautious step onto the lavender carpet, she signaled for Eller to follow. The purple-and-blue walls curved upward into a recessed ceiling, from which more chandeliers dangled, sparkled and swayed.

Eller tiptoed behind, eyes darting around the hallway. Sariya's hand dragged along the depressed granite wall. Portraits of lords encased in shimmering frames hung from each side, every pompous face displaying an identical scoff.

A hollow rapping echoed through the hall—and grew louder by the tap. Footsteps approached. Eller gasped and darted forward, taking cover behind a shimmering velvet curtain.

"What are you doing?" Sariya tried not to yell.

"Hiding. Someone's coming." The footsteps drew near.

Sariya snapped, "Get out from there. I can still see your feet, you bloody fool!"

The curtain flowed in violet-and-sapphire waves when Eller peeked from behind, realizing much of his body was visible. "Good thinking. Follow me!" He lunged from the cover of the curtain and squeezed behind the suit of armor in the recessed pocket of the hall.

"Will you get out from there?" Voices echoed with the footsteps. "There's nowhere to hide. Just walk beside me."

Eller's head poked over the suit's pauldron. The voices became distinct. Encroaching shadows rounded the corner.

"Now!"

His eyes fell to the floor, and he bolted toward her.

"Walk by me side," she said with a firm nod. "And wipe away the look of shame. Stand tall. Look like you belong." Two women rounded the corner. "And let me do the talking."

Sariya strode along, her chest out and chin held high. The two women walked toward them, their words fading to whispers. One of them wore a flowing scarlet dress. Her hard-sole boots met the thin lavender carpet like stone on stone. The other woman wore black dress slacks and a matching silken tailcoat. A corset squeezed her chest, held together by ornate golden buckles.

The pirates passed the women by without drawing more than a curious glance. Sariya, grinned, celebrating her passive confidence. 'There we go. Hiding in plain—'

"Excuse me!" one of the women shouted. "Where do the two of you think you're going?"

"Damn it," Sariya whispered, biting her lip. She turned around with a forced smile. "Well pardon us, m'ladies. We were called in to do some final diagnostics on the *Sky Guard*. And we seem to have gotten lost."

The woman in the tailcoat crossed her arms. Her tall grey figure left a grim shadow upon the wall. "I wasn't notified of anyone else coming in tonight."

Sariya shrugged. "We just got our orders from the boss about an hour ago. Usually she walks us up." She put her hands in her belt and chuckled. "You gotta understand, we don't often get to wander the halls of grand castles—given our lowly Vandeni upbringings."

The woman in the dress overpowered Sariya's laugh with her own. "Just to the right of the hallway in front of you, dearies. Then make a left at the second staircase. The ship is docked at the top of the tower."

The tailcoated woman leaned over the other's shoulder. The hallway's echo carried her words. "Should I verify their identities?"

"No need," the woman in the dress said. She looked to Sariya and smiled. "This one looks familiar to me. I have seen her in these halls before." Her long, stiff finger pointed down the hall. "Go on. We do not wish to keep you from your labor."

"We appreciate your direction, kind misses." Sariya bowed her head. She walked away, holding her breath, and Eller followed.

She did not let herself exhale until she heard the retreat of their hollow steps. The woman in the tailcoat shouted, "Be sure your credentials are in order." Sariya's spine tingled at her words. "The guards will not permit you entrance without them."

Eller and Sariya rounded the corner. The floor turned from carpet to stone. Athenis' setting light gleamed through arched windows, melding with the blue eminence of the chandeliers.

"By the fury of the sea, that was close," Eller said, hand over his heart.

"Indeed, matey." Her boots clacked on the floor. "But what do I always say? Composure is the best cover."

His blinking eyes rolled to her. "You never say that."

"But I will now."

He glanced over his shoulder. "She recognized you. The one in the dress."

"Aye," Sariya said with a nod. "Probably from when I was a young lass. Luckily, she couldn't place me."

"What do we do about the guards when we get up top?"

"Either take them out or sneak around 'em." She smiled. "It doesn't concern me much."

The curling stairwell seemed to never end. 'How did I used to *run* all the way up when I was a girl?' she thought, drawing heavy breaths. 'You'd think they'd consider installing an elevator at some point.'

The stairwell led to a curved hallway. Wide windows adorned each wall, giving view to the rest of the castle on one side and the lights of Sea Haven on another. Athenis' final light clung to the horizon before it would drown beneath the sea. Some fifteen hours later, it would be reborn in the east.

The hallway coiled the tower. Sariya looked out the window—there she was. A massive metal vessel's nose curved upward, displaying the golden crest of Denavoss. The armor was a grey-silver, giving a dull reflection but bearing no glimmer or shine. Glossy windows curled over the grand bridge, near the *Sky Guard*'s bow.

As the pirates rounded the hall, more of the ship came into view. A massive turret rested on the top deck. Brass pipelines swirled along the sloped keel. Two electro-sails towered high, and a pair of sonic thrusters protruded from the back.

"Sariya..." Eller's voice trembled. "The captain designed this?"

"He did." Her hand dragged along the window. "Every plate of armor, every power transfer cylinder, every cabin, every detail from the frame to the sails." She shook her head. "Katrielle exercised no restraint in stealing from his blueprints."

As the hallway curved on, the windows gave view to a gangway. Sariya looked through the windows. The gangway served as the ship's dock. Drawing nearer, she saw the guards. They were not common security officers. They were tall, hulking men in shimmering armor. Their ornate, expressionless helmets held a steadfast intensity.

"Oh no," Eller said. His feet dragged on the floor. "Imperial knights."

"It's fine," Sariya said with a half smirk. "We can just climb over the top."

"No, we can't. There are windows everywhere. They'll see us."

"Then we'll take them out. They'll never know what hit 'em." She reached for her shock-cannon.

Eller grabbed her wrist. "Are you crazy?!" He turned around to see if anyone had followed. "Have you ever seen an Imperial knight in battle before? There is no fiercer a foe."

"No. But I know that they don't use shock-cannons. That'll give us a leg up, wouldn't ye say?"

Eller shook his head. "Only the most orthodox of them don't use shock-cannons. And even if these happen to be two highly devout Imperial servicemen, they wield swords that draw and avert shock-cannon fire."

Sariya's eyes widened. "Really?" She leaned forward, jaw gaping. "Why don't we use those?"

"Yeah right. I tried lifting one a few years back. They're heavy as hell and awkward to handle. Using one of those swords requires years of training and thousands of platinum in strength implants."

"Okay, I got it." Sariya stopped and placed her hand over Eller's chest. "I'll draw their fire, and you go around and shoot them in the back. If we overwhelm them, a few shots are bound to get through."

"Sariya." Eller's wide palms embraced her hands. "Listen to me. They are elite warriors. They'll cut me like a fresh fillet if I try to get behind them. Even if I did, their armor is cybernetically designed to withstand shock-cannon fire. Sleeper bolts won't take them down."

A twisted smile formed on her face. "Then we'll set our pistols to kill."

"Sariya!"

"I'm kidding. I'm just kidding."

He moaned. She chuckled. "Okay," Sariya said. "We can't fight them. And we can't sneak around them. What ye have in mind, matey?"

"We get them away from the door." Eller's chestnut eyes glistened through his lashes. "We'll try to hack the control panel or weld through the lock."

"Get them away... from the door," Sariya said with a slight frown. "And how do ye plan on doing that?"

"*You* are going to do what you do best, Sariya Vaeliz," he said with a crooked smile. "Talk."

V. A Daring Plan (or Lack Thereof)

"Hello, sirs." Sariya crossed her hands behind her back, a childish bounce in her stance. "Reporting for repairs on the *Sky Guard*."

"I didn't know anyone else was coming on today," one of the knights said. The golden filigree of his silver armor spiraled over his pauldrons and formed the shape of a striking cougar on his torso.

The other knight's armor was a dull chrome and bore no ornate decoration. "You will have to show us your credentials, miss." His sharp metal finger extended. "No one enters the vessel without display of credentials. You know this."

"Oh, yes. Of course." Sariya reached into her jacket pocket. "Where'd I put that data system? Gotta be around here somewhere." She looked up at the knights with a nervous cackle. "Damn, ye know what, lads? I must've left it with me partner. He should be up shortly. Probably best that I wait for him anyway. Don't want to bother the two of ye to open the door twice."

"We can wait," said the dull-armored knight with a stiff nod.

"If there's one virtue of an Imperial knight that I know not to question, it's patience." She stepped toward them. "So, how's your evening treating ya, good sirs?"

"That's close enough. Thank you." The golden-armored knight outstretched his hand.

Sariya shrugged and chuckled. "The two of ye can't be afraid of a lil' Rogue lass like me, can ye?"

"Just following protocol, miss." The dull-armored knight's fingers caressed the hilt of his sword.

"Protocol." Sariya leaned against the window. Her shoulder squeaked, sliding down the glass. "I know all about protocol, my gallant friends. Trying to get this hunk of steel up in the air for Madame Denavoss has been a nightmare."

The golden-armored knight nodded. "I have heard that your team has had some difficulties."

"Difficulties don't begin to describe it. We've had to repair not one but two charge crystal chambers. So of course, we had to replace the surrounding coils and several transfer cylinders as well." Sariya rolled her eyes and gave an exasperated sigh. "To put it bluntly, lads, it's been a little taste of electric hell."

"It sure does sound like it."

"Oh my—and the artillery. Don't even get me started on the artil—"

"You look familiar," the dull-armored knight interrupted.

"Well sure I do, sire." She laughed and maintained a relaxed stance, though her heart raced. "I've been working on this ship. You've probably seen me passing—"

He interrupted once more. "No, no. That is not what I am referring to. It's your smile." He stepped closer. Sariya swallowed. Muffled words resonated from behind his helm. "You would not happen to be *related* to Lady Denavoss, would you?"

Sariya laughed and shook her head. "Oh, how I wish that be the case, sire." 'Come on, Eller. Hurry up,' she thought. "If I were, she wouldn't have me working so hard." She licked her lips and glanced over her shoulder.

"But you do not bear so much of a resemblance to Madame Katrielle. More of one to Madame—"

With those words, Eller sprinted past the hall with his shock-cannon drawn. "Get down!" one of the knights yelled. But before they could intervene, Eller fired a thundering blast through the corridor that struck the window near Sariya's face.

Her arms flailed and she went down. The dull-armored knight sprang to action. "Intruder! Assassin!" He darted down the corridor after Eller. The golden-armored knight followed, but the other knight raised his fist. "Tend to her!" he shouted, pointing to Sariya. "I'll deal with this deranged offender!"

Sariya took shallow breaths and tensed her muscles, forcing her body to quiver and shake.

"Oh, by the Guardians!" The knight knelt and took hold of Sariya's hand. "You're still alive. He probably didn't have his cannon set to kill. You should be okay."

She breathed shallowly. Her eyes widened and flooded with tears as she looked upon the knight's shining helm.

"Don't you die on me!" He placed his hands over her chest and began compressions. Sariya coughed and squealed, hoping that his strength would not crack her ribs. She held her breath and let her eyes fall to a near-shut squint.

"No! Stay with me, miss!"

Through her lashes, Sariya saw the knight remove his helmet. He was an attractive man. A strong jawline, high cheekbones—thick waves of dark grey hair complimented his dazzling grey eyes. Receiving the kiss of life from this noble knight would not be such a horrible fate.

As he leaned toward her, Sariya reached for her pistol and delivered a shock-cannon blast to his head. The electric beams fizzled across his face. He looked to her in writhing confusion before falling unconscious. Perhaps their courtship could continue on another occasion.

She pulled herself up with a groan and pushed her hair behind her ears. She looked down the hall—no sign of backup security. But no sign of Eller either. "C'mon, Eller," she whispered. "You said you could lose him. Get back here. I don't know how these Imperial security systems work."

She aimed her pistol down the hall with one hand and tapped the security panel with the other. "Let's see. It requires a code or facial scan. I wonder if I can..." She scrolled to a black screen, overflowing with hundreds of codes. "Ah-hah. The encryption screen. If I can bypass the protocols, I can access the system's base code—"

An alarm sounded. Sariya gasped. "Oh hell, did I do that?" The screen went black, then flashed red.

"Attention personnel!" a staticky voice said over the loudspeaker. "We have an intruder on the premises. Use any force necessary to apprehend."

'*Eller* did that.' He had insisted they maintain transmission silence, but she had to check his status. "Eller, where are you?" She pressed the communication device to her ear, hoping to hear at least a hushed reply. "If I wait here much longer, I'll be compromised. If you've evaded capture, tell me now!"

No response. Voices shouted over the ringing alarm. With a tight grip on the handle of her pistol, she moved to the other end of the hall and looked upward through the window. "Eller, I can make it out the side of the hall and over the top of the gangway. But I need to know your status, matey!"

"Go!" Eller's directive pierced her eardrum with sharp feedback. "Get moving. I'll be right behind ya."

"What if ye don't make it?"

"Then you'll have to come rescue me."

More screams circled the halls—followed by shock-cannon fire. It was now or never. She reached for her belt and drew her rapier. After she flipped a switch under its side, the blade ignited with a web of electricity. With a faint thrust, the sharp edge sizzled against the window. Shattering glass plummeted below.

She leaned out and looked to the top of the gangway. Could she *really* jump to the top? The height was not a problem, but the ledge was curved and steep—impossible to grab hold of. She looked down. Broken glass crashed into the roaring shoreline.

A nervous tension seeped from her mind. She shook the sensation out of her fingertips and expelled her panic with a rapid breath. Sariya shut her eyes and pictured the curve of the outer wall. Where could she grab hold? What was the flattest piece of the structure?

The top of the windowsill.

She sprinted forward at an angle, toward the side of the window. When the floor receded from peripheral view, she leapt. Airborne over the surf break, she reached for the top of the gangway. Her hands touched the grey metal, but gravity pulled the rest of her body down.

She flung to the side, and the soles of her boots tapped the bottom ledge. Using her momentum to leap, she reached forward as she ascended. Her arms embraced the top of the structure. Pulling herself up, she twisted around and landed on her back.

Her heart pounded through her chest. With a dry cackle, she surged to her feet. There was no time to rest or celebrate. Sariya sprinted across the top of the gangway. The stars took their place in the amethyst-and-sapphire night sky. The dueling moons rested in crescent form above the *Sky Guard*.

"Eller!" Sariya yelled over her communication system. "I had to jump at an angle and hurl myself over the ledge to get up here. Think you can manage? Or do ye want me to see if I can open the door from the other side?"

"Are you crazy?!" His voice shrieked into the device. "Of course I want you to open the door! I'm being chased and shot at by half a dozen angry Imperials. Do you really think I'm going to be able to figure out *exactly* how you jumped out a window without killing yourself?"

"Point taken, mate." She neared the end of the gangway and hurtled over the taffrail. Her boots clanked on the sturdy metal of the *Sky Guard*'s top deck. She turned around. Across the darkness, within Sea Haven Castle, flashes of weaponized electricity ignited the hallway. Between flashes, she saw the shape of a man fleeing from oncoming bolts.

'I'll get ye out of there, Eller,' she thought. She ran to the nearest set of stairs and sprinted to the top deck. Turning toward the ship's front, she made for the bridge.

"Any luck getting that door open?" Eller asked. "Should I make for the gangway?"

"Not even on the bridge yet, El."

The sound of shock-cannon fire thundered through the speaker. "Well, if you could do that sometime soon, that'd be great. I'm running out of places to hide."

She climbed up the stairway and went to open the door to the bridge. It was locked. "Oh, damn it all to hell."

She flinched when a thought came to her: Eller's method of entering the castle. She reached for her utility tool and activated the weld setting. The blue flame ignited as Sariya melted the silver encasing around the lock.

She gasped in sudden panic, pulling the tool away from the scorching metal. "You bloody fool," she whispered. This was no makeshift lock, like the one Eller broke along the cliffs. This was no ordinary door; it was her father's design. If she melted the digital panel, an emergency lock would seal the door. The ship would go into high-security mode and an alarm would sound.

With a nervous rush of adrenaline, she banged the window. "Why is there no back door?!" Her head swiveled to the lock. A back door—Captain Bellacor always left a back door. Behind the smoking opening of the security panel, there were three glass encasings sheltering weak channels of electricity. If the captain had designed this door's security system as he had the *Ocean Flame*'s, Sariya had a way in.

She held her breath and allowed the blue flame of the welder to brush the lock's power transfer cylinders. She had to break the two outside encasings while leaving the middle tube intact.

The glass melted and the electric beams flowed freely. Sweat poured down her brow, sparks stung her face. The metal latches beneath the electric streams smoldered orange. With a hollow click, the door budged free. She kicked it open and ran onto the bridge.

Arching windows offered a wraparound view from sky to sea. The entire upper level of the vessel was visible—from port to starboard, stern to bow.

Sariya took a seat at the control panel. Her fingers flipped switches and pressed buttons in a frantic frenzy. "C'mon, power. Where are ye?"

A deep rumble quaked from the bottom of the ship. Red, purple and green lights flickered to life. Hissing voltage crawled through walls and into the bronze power transfer cylinders. The glass viewing panes of the cylinders ignited with flowing currents of electricity.

Her hands came together for a single celebratory clap. "Okay, okay." Sariya cycled through the green screen of the data system. "Takeoff procedure!" She followed the digital path—"Gangway release!"—and leaned forward to press the icon.

"Eller," she said, speaking through her communication system. "I have the door open. Get yerself over here."

"Start taking off!"

"Eller, you're not aboard yet!"

"If you wait for me, they'll follow me aboard. You have to take off."

"Well scurry to the gangway. Maybe you can still make it."

"Copy."

Sariya tapped the flashing "Takeoff" icon. The screen read "Please confirm identity or enter launch codes."

"Launch codes," Sariya uttered with a solemn bow of her head. "Sariya, you bloody fool. How did ye forget about launch codes?" Her eyes widened with a clever idea as she looked to the screen. "Identity confirmation: Sariya Vaeliz."

"ACCESS DENIED!" the screen was quick to reply.

"Damn ye, cyberdemon." She tapped the red icon marked "Emergency Takeoff" at the bottom of the screen. "'Nothing's ever easy for a Vaeliz, Father always said."

A warning message appeared on the data system: "Emergency takeoff will limit many of the ship's functions to minimal baseline. Sending distress signal."

"No, no! Don't send a distress signal!" She collapsed over the control panel. "Or just go ahead. I don't care anymore." She straightened and took the helm. With a forceful pull of the wheel, she brought the ship starboard, undocking from the gangway. With a final glance to the tunnel, she saw Eller. The *Ocean Flame*'s third mate sprinted down the hall, a crowd of Imperials at his rear.

His hands flailed in a ferocious manner. "Go! Go!" he yelled.

Sariya did as instructed. She continued to pull away while angling the rear of the ship toward the gangway. She rushed to the control panel and took control of the turret. 'Luckily the emergency takeoff sequence didn't completely shut down weaponry,' she thought. She could fire low energy blasts. That is all she would need.

Eller reached the end of the tunnel and jumped across the gap. As he hurtled through midair, Sariya's stomach turned upside down. 'I'm out too far!' she thought. 'He's not going to make it.'

But her commanding officer slammed into the top deck, rolling on his side.

"Yes!" Sariya yelled as she pushed the thrusters forward. The ship accelerated to the fastest speed that the emergency protocol would allow. She shuffled back to the control panel and fired a shot from the turret. A weak beam of lightning launched from the large weapon. It passed between the *Sky Guard* and the tunnel, striking the cliffs below—as she intended. She set the weapon to automatically continue firing, forcing the Imperial pursuers to halt at the edge. Their path to the *Sky Guard* was blocked.

Sariya raised a fist. With a roaring laugh, she leapt in triumph.

As the ship pulled away from Sea Haven, artillery fired from the castle. The dim lights flickered overhead. The vessel shook with each pounding blast of electricity.

"Oh no, we need to go faster!" Sariya pushed the accelerator with both hands, but the electro-sail's power output was limited by the emergency flight mode.

Two Imperial attack ships rose from behind the castle, closing in on the large vessel. "Commandeers of the *Sky Guard*," a deep Imperial accent said through the loudspeaker. "Land the vessel immediately. Or we'll send her to the depths with your pirate carcasses still aboard."

Sariya put a hand on her transmission device. "Eller, I know you're probably exhausted after that lil' chase you found yerself in. But I'm going to need you on the bridge, matey." The angled body and curved wings of one of the attack ships rocketed by the bridge, firing high-powered blasts of electricity upon the vessel's upper deck. "Now!"

Sea Haven Castle faded behind rising mist. The Imperial attack ships circled the *Sky Guard*, firing upon her hull.

Eller burst through the door. Sweat drenched his brow. "Sariya, they're trying to bring down the ship. Return fire!"

She pulled tight on the helm. "Matey, I'd love to. But I can barely get her to *turn* while in this damned emergency mode, much less ready the cannons."

The vessel rocked, struck by another volley from the attack ships. "So, override it!" Eller yelled, leaning over the control panel to her left.

"I don't know how!"

"Have you ever even flown an airship before?"

"No!" She erupted with unruly laughter, then pushed the joystick to the right of the helm forward. The *Sky Guard* fell in rapid descent. Eller tumbled over the console. "But I do like it thus far."

"What are you doing?" Eller pointed out the window. "You're going to crash us into the sea."

"Nah, mate. I'll pull up and they'll be the ones who'll find themselves swimming." The Imperials trailed the *Sky Guard*'s descent. Her eyes flashed in the electric fusillade raining from their attack ships.

Eller tapped the green screen of the console. "Sariya, they can recover faster than we can. They're in small maneuverable craft. We're in a gigantic cruiser."

"Aye, good point." She pulled up on the joystick, leveling their course.

The green screen's interface shifted. Eller shuffled through menus and icons, typing in code. "Ah-hah," he said. The console gave a lively beep. Overhead lights brightened. The roar of the vessel's electro-sail deepened.

"Emergency mode disengaged. Full function restored," the screen's reading said.

"Yes! You did it, mate." A surge of terror interrupted Sariya's triumphant laughter when the Imperial ships fired upon the bridge.

"Bring the ship down this instant," one of their voices said through the transmission system. "Or we will increase firepower."

Eller straightened. "Give me the helm."

"Aye." Sariya nodded and stepped back.

"Take control of the artillery." He pointed to the nearby control panel. "You have to take those attack ships down. There are only two. It would take a long time for their cannons to do us any severe damage, but they'll remain engaged until support arrives. And the last thing we want is to be swarmed by Imperial fighters."

She stepped to the console. "Aye. We take them out before more grunts follow their signal to us." She pressed an icon, which granted her control of the main batteries. No longer hindered by low power output, she charged up the front and rear cannons.

"Not too high." His dark eyes followed her hands. "We want to disable their ships, not kill them."

She nodded.

"Now," Eller said with a slight smirk. "Let's see what this thing can do."

He drove the throttle forward. Sariya braced herself. The electro-sail was propelled by a booming explosion. Her eyelids peeled back as the floor trembled beneath her boots.

With euphoric laughter, Eller and Sariya looked ahead. Carving a path through the mist, the vessel left the Imperial attack ships trailing behind. The two small craft increased their speed to keep up.

Sariya swiveled the rear cannon. Her finger jolted over the blue button atop the joystick. With vengeful thunder, the battery fired upon the two crafts clustered in tight formation. The fighters peeled away, one in a sharp bank and the other in a barrel roll.

Sariya pressed the transmission button. "Doesn't feel too good to be seeing a bolt of cannon fire heading your way, does it, my sweet lil' knightly chaps?"

As she snickered, Eller shoved her hand away from the button. "Don't talk to them," he said, eyes ahead. "Shoot them down."

She nodded and swiveled the cannons toward the attack ships. "Hey, El," she said with a grin. "I'm really glad that you're here."

"That makes one of us."

One of the ships surfaced from under the nose of the *Sky Guard*. The pilot's voice crackled through the bridge speakers. "This is the end for you, pirate filth." Streaming blasts of electricity launched from his ship, wrapping the bridge in a cocoon of white-and-purple voltage.

The blinding light burned an impression on Sariya's eyes. The vessel circled for another attack run. She swiveled the front cannon along its path. When the vessel swung wide toward the *Sky Guard*, Sariya fired. The high-powered beam launched from the turret and struck the wing of the attack ship. Electricity ravaged the small fighter's armor. In a flat spin, the smoking aircraft fell toward the sea.

"Hah! That's one!" Sariya's voice cracked with her rejoicing.

"Hell yeah. Good work." Eller adjusted the ship's course twenty degrees left. "Now get the other one."

"On it."

As the second fighter craft moved to attack the airship's broadside, Sariya fired both cannons, hoping to catch her enemy in crossfire. But the small vessel dived low in an evasive spin.

The snarling female voice of the pilot entered the bridge's speaker via transmission. "Put the vessel in the water. An entire squadron is en route to drown your vessel in firepower. They will make short work of you. Do not resign yourselves to death. Surrender now, and I will inform the Imperial courts of your cooperative nature." A volley of blasts shook the ship's underside. "The choice is yours."

"Take her down!" Eller barked.

Sariya pressed a button on the terminal. "Hold on. I'm trying to access the underside turret." The monitor turned to a digital feed that displayed the belly of the ship. "Okay, got it."

The Imperial fighter came into sight. Sariya discharged weaponized lightning from the lower turret. The Imperial pilot returned fire. After a short volley, the underside cannon froze in an unresponsive state.

"Damn!" Sariya said.

Eller looked over. "What is it?"

"She disabled the lower cannon. Maintenance must not have been complete." Another series of cannon fire shook the ship's underside. Sariya held the terminal to keep balance. "I'm going to go into the artillery bay and take her out with the side cannons. You just keep her floating, okay?"

"Sure!" Eller said with enthused sarcasm. "I'll just fly this giant frigate by myself. Don't mind me."

"I shan't be gone long, mate." Sariya pressed a green icon near the back of the bridge. A small elevator rose from the floor with a mechanical purr. "You're my hero!" The lift brought her to the lower deck.

Mechanized electronic noise surrounded the dull metal tunnels of the subdeck. The blue lights shuttered with the Imperial fighter's blasts on the vessel. Sariya ran down the hall. Greasy, burning smells poured into her breath. An automatic door opened as she approached.

She reached the artillery bay. Rows of shock-turrets lay mounted on each side. They could be controlled manually or via the data system at the central terminal. She ran to the terminal and tapped the screen. The Imperial fighter soared by the window, firing as it passed.

"I've had enough of you," Sariya whispered with a grin. She unleashed a barrage of cannon fire from the port side of the ship.

The fighter keeled right and took cover behind the *Sky Guard*'s stern, assaulting the electro-sail and rear thrusters.

Sariya switched to the two rear cannons and took aim.

But the cruiser pulled up and out of her range before she could fire.

She stomped the grated metal floor. 'You're smarter than your wingman, ain't ye?'

An idea struck the mind of the young pirate. "Eller," she said over her communication system.

"Aye?"

"Fire at her from the main batteries." She eyed the sets of turrets on each side of the bay. "Then tell me which way she's moving to evade."

Eller cleared his throat. "You want me to fly the ship *and* man the main cannons... *and* navigate?"

"I do."

He did not respond. But the airship shook with the thunderous resonance of the main batteries' bombardment. "Starboard!" Eller's scream crackled in Sariya's ear. "She's breaking starboard!"

Sariya sprinted from the middle terminal to one of the starboard cannons—the second from the left. She had always preferred firing a cannon manually to using a central system.

The fighter's voltaic reverberations shook the floor. The electric streak of its sonic thrusters flashed in the corner of Sariya's eye. Her thumbs brushed against the cold metal of the bronze turret. She felt the weight in her biceps as she grasped the handles and aimed upward. Her mind and body merged with the sizzling vibration of its electric power.

She fired four shots. The fighter returned fire. The final of Sariya's blasts struck the tip of her enemy's wing. The attack ship twirled, plummeting in electric overflow.

The small ship fell out of sight—but a moment later, glided back into view. The wing was smoking. Sparks discharged from the attack ship, and it swayed from side to side.

'She can't keep her level,' Sariya thought with a half-smile.

The Imperial fighter slowed and fell back, pulling away from the *Sky Guard*. Sariya activated her communication device. "Eller, she's pulling away! She's retreating."

"No, Sariya," Eller was quick to reply. "You compromised her. She's pulling *back*. But she's still following us. She'll keep on our tail until backup arrives."

Sariya ran to the central terminal and looked to the rearview digital monitor. "Damn, you're right!" she said, seeing the stubborn fighter on the screen.

She had an idea. Not an idea, a memory—something that her father had presented when she was a little girl: a long-range missile in the *Sky Guard*'s blueprints. 'By the grace of the Guardians please be there. Please say that the missile isn't the one contraption that the House of Denavoss forewent to save coin.' She navigated the digital screen, pausing on an icon that gave her a wide grin. The icon read "Long-Range Voltage Missile."

"Slow the ship down."

Eller responded with cynicism. "Slow her down? Our only hope is outrunning that damaged fighter. And you want to slow down?"

"Yes. I'm going to hit her with a voltage missile. She's too far away. I need you to decelerate, matey."

"Alright," Eller said with a sigh. "Be sure not to give it too much power. You'll fry her if you turn it up too high."

"Aye." She lowered the power output to medium.

The *Sky Guard*'s roaring machinery calmed. Sariya leaned over the screen. The green glow absorbed her viridian eyes. A yellow circle hovered over the digital projection of the Imperial ship's shape, accompanied by a triplet of beeps. "C'mon... a little slower, El." The fighter grew larger on the screen; the circle's enveloping borders expanded around its jagged body. The beeps quickened. "C'mon... c'mon..."

The yellow circle turned red, locking the attack ship within its borders. The tripling beeps turned into a solid tone. Sariya pulled the blue trigger on the joystick, firing the missile. The screen displayed a spiraling torpedo of voltage.

Sariya ran to the starboard side and leaned over the window. She could not see the missile. With a groan, she ran back to the central terminal. She zoomed in on the rear monitor. The missile was out of sight, but she could see the attack ship. She held her breath. In a blinding flash, an electric eruption stretched over the screen. The attack ship stalled and declined toward the sea.

"Yes!" Sariya shouted and leapt high. "We hit her!" But her celebration halted when she observed the nosediving ship. There was no parachute. Why was there no parachute?

"C'mon, lass. Get out of there." Sariya's fists clenched. "Eject, damn it. Eject!" Tears formed beneath her eyelids.

The canopy popped off, and a parachute appeared. The horrible sinking feeling washed away. Sariya took a deep breath, which turned into a resigned moan. She smiled and closed her eyes, crossing her hands in front of her lips. "Guardians, protect her," she whispered with a sniffle. "Rytekos, allow her passage through your shapeless sea. Shal, give strength to her mind and will. Haelovar, guide her back to the peaceful comfort of her Imperial home."

"Sariya," Eller said via transmission. "Good work down there. But you're gunna wanna sit down. We're going sailing."

Sariya cuffed her ear. "Why not just stay in the air? We'll move much faster."

"They'll be activating the satellites to try and track us."

Sariya felt the negative gravitational force in her thighs as the ship descended.

Eller spoke again. "They won't be able to lock onto us easily if we're in the water."

"Aye."

The vessel rocked in turbulence as she looked for a seat. The electrical purrs within the power transfer cylinders rose in pitch.

"Well, give me a second here, would ya, mate?"

As the ship declined, the turbulence increased. Sariya plopped down in a chair at the central terminal and strapped herself in.

VI. Family Affairs

With a loud crash, the *Sky Guard* landed in the water. Sariya's body jolted forward into the crossing safety straps. Red emergency lights flashed. Rapid warning tones echoed across the subdeck. The ship tilted to portside, creaking and groaning. After all that Sariya had done to obtain her, the vessel was going to capsize.

At a steep angle, the *Sky Guard* halted and swayed starboard. With a second crash, the ship corrected itself and found balance. Seawater sprayed the windows with a welcoming mist.

"Whew." Sariya unstrapped herself from the seat and slouched back. "Eller," she said with a groan. "Not your best landing."

"This thing is not meant to be landed at high speeds, Sariya. I did my best."

"I know ye did, mate."

Eller's bashful grin melted into his words. "Good shooting back there. Why don't you work with the artillery crew more often?"

"Because Eller"—her brow rose—"artillery is boring when you're not in battle."

They shared a chuckle.

"I'm going to switch us to low power. At least until we get out of Imperial waters," Eller said. "I don't want any search parties to lock onto our signal."

"Aye. Good thinkin', mate."

"It's about to get a little dark down there." The transmission turned to static. "Why don't you go check for stowaways? Crew members or maintenance workers that got stuck on the engineering deck. If we have any unexpected passengers, we can send them out on the auxiliary craft. The last thing we want is for someone to send a distress signal."

"On it, mate." Sariya stood. Bright blue lights overhead and on the walls faded to dim vermillion. The droning voltage in the pipes softened to an undulant hum. Automated systems within the walls fell silent. "Oh," she said with a sudden idea. "Eller, look for a camouflaging mechanism on the main console. I know my father wanted to implement one. But the tech wasn't available yet."

"Let's see here," he said before the transmission turned to static. "Nope. Nope. Maybe? What does this do?" A pitchy, strained scrape echoed between the walls. "Well, that did something. Let me take a look." Sariya smiled at the youthful curiosity in his voice. "Oh my—Sariya! The hull is changing color like an Imperial's skin in a harsh winter!"

Sariya ran to the window. "Beautiful," she said. "Black as shadow. Purple as the sea." Though the *Sky Guard*'s darkened armor was not invisible to enemy eyes, her reflection and shape would be *less* visible. At least, that was the idea.

"I'm heading off to check the engineering deck," she said, stepping away from the window.

"Don't take too long. I need a navigator up here."

"Sit tight, mate. I'll make haste."

She giggled, scurrying across the artillery bay. "We did it," the young pirate whispered to herself. "We actually did it." The sound of deep-sea waves collapsing upon the hull brought a feathery lightness to her mind and soul. "We took the *Sky Guard*." She swung her arms, taking one more look at the artillery bay. "We took it for you, Father." She nodded at the rows of shock-turrets, thanking them for their service in her battle with the Imperial attack ships.

She pranced through the hallway. The low-powered rows of reddish lights guided her path, dim enough to avoid radar tracking. She smiled at her father's brilliant design, hurrying down the spiraling stairs. Like a child inspirited by the shine of morning, she leapt from step to step.

At the engineering deck, the constant pounding, chafing smells and blinding electrical light would have deterred some, but not Sariya Vaeliz. She covered her mouth, holding back an eager scream.

Hundreds of pipes channeled electrical energy from bulky canisters. The cannisters held massive blue charge crystals, soaked in a renewable current of radiant voltage. Streams of electricity traveled through the coils and into the transfer cylinders, powering the entire ship.

Sariya drew her pistol, peering behind machinery and under consoles. "Hello," she called out, distracted by the neon lights, shiny levers and dancing electricity. "Any workers left aboard?" She crept along a wall, her pistol aimed forward. "I ain't gunna hurt ye, mates. Not all pirates are to be feared, ye know." She looked to the railing on the upper walkway. Oh, how the *Ocean Flame*'s engineering crew would enjoy exploring this deck. "Some of us are quite friendly if you just give us a good laugh and a bottle of whisky."

She made several circles. The area was clear. 'Not the best news either. We could have conscripted an engineer for the voyage,' Sariya thought. 'If something goes awry, Eller will have to fix it and I'll have to take the helm.' She shrugged. 'Who am I kidding? That actually sounds fun.' She took a deep breath and reined in her thoughts. 'Actually, I've put the poor chap through enough today.'

After navigating the halls, she took the elevator down to the first level above the orlop deck. "Crew quarters," she whispered. "Let's have a look."

The rooms were spacious. The beds were large, and the thick walls offered more privacy than any corner of the *Ocean Flame*. 'This must be the officers' quarters,' Sariya thought. But there were too many rooms. No ship would ever have this many commissioned officers.

'This is the crew quarters!' As she walked by the bedrooms, a smile fell on her face. She imagined Thraeliss and Dorgallik fighting over which of them got to hang their trophies on the wall. Her smile turned to laughter when she looked to the common room, picturing the navigation crew sitting across from the engineering crew. She could hear their mugs clanking, their dice hitting the glossy grey table, coins exchanging hands and playful insults being exchanged.

She did not know why, but her vibrant grin remained when she entered the officer's quarters. She thought of Halsik plopping on the large bed, overworked and able to snore through the night in his private cabin.

There was no one there. She had patrolled the crew and officer quarters three times, looking under beds, inside closets and within the showers. They were alone.

She took the elevator back to the main deck. Her skin turned to goosebumps as she felt the briny wind on her face. The towers of the front and rear electro-sails propelled the enormous vessel with weak bursts of lightning. The ship's armor, still in black-and-purple camouflage, hid in the shadows while treading the sea with pride.

'It's yours, Father,' Sariya thought, admiring the intricate design. 'It's all yours.'

She stepped up the stairs to the bridge and pushed open the door that she had unlocked with her welder.

"Oh, good," Eller said with an elated sigh. "You're back."

Sariya approached and rested her hand on his shoulder. "I'm back!"

"Did you have fun exploring?"

"I wasn't exploring!" she said, crossing her arms. "I was clearing the area like ye said, mate."

Eller's eyes slanted toward her, a smug grin on his face.

"Okay, I may have been exploring a little."

He gave a heckling chuckle, turning forward. "Is she as amazing as she looks?"

Sariya nodded. "Her magnificence isn't done justice by view of the hull alone."

"I can't wait to see for myself," Eller said. He pointed toward the chair to his left. "Take a seat. I really need a navigator."

"Aye." Sariya sat in the chair, looking at the map on the screen.

"How's our course?"

She squinted over the yellow monitor, reading the data in the corner. She followed the trajectory that the system had calculated for the *Sky Guard*. "You could probably adjust us five degrees west. We'll have more of a chance of catching up to the *Ocean Flame* that way."

"I'm just making for the Vanden Reaches for now," Eller said. He adjusted the helm to match Sariya's suggested course. "We can make contact with the *Ocean Flame* once we're clear of Imperial waters. Worse comes to worst, we can just meet them in Rogue Haven."

Sariya nodded and checked the map for any sign of stormy weather. "Sounds like a plan, mate." The skies appeared clear along their current course.

"So, no stowaways?" Eller asked.

"Nope." She glanced his way and shrugged. "I circled the engineering deck and crew quarters several times. Looks like it's just us, mate."

"There *is* one place that you failed to check... captain's quarters."

Sariya and Eller jumped at the sound of the slow-burning words spoken with an Imperial accent.

"Keep still," the female voice spoke again. "Stay in those seats or I will open fire."

Sariya glanced back. A tall, slender woman stood at the doorway in side-laced slacks, a white-and-gold corset and a matching silken cloak flowing from her shoulders to the ground. She held a golden pistol with a slim handle and a robust barrel. The weapon featured engravings of fine floral details. Its aim shifted between Eller and Sariya.

"Madame Katrielle Denavoss." Sariya snarled as she spoke the name.

The woman looked down on the young pirate with a smile whiter than her wardrobe. "Hello, cousin."

Her icy blonde hair held faint, pale shades of blue and fell in thick waves over her shoulders. Golden earrings with green gems dangled from her lobes. A matching necklace rested on the column of her throat. "An impressive stunt that the two of you have pulled." Her platinum lipstick gleamed with her slight smile. "But it's over now."

"Eller," Sariya whispered. "Block any distress signal she tries to put out."

Eller's brow furrowed. His eyes darted around the room.

"Do not bother." Katrielle reached into her blouse and flashed her mobile data system with a limp wrist. "The signal has already been transmitted, Sariya." Her long nails tapped the small screen. "My own *personal* code. The Imperial military will have already locked on. They

shouldn't be far behind. And they'll have a whole squadron this time."
An arrogant smirk overtook her pursed lips.

"What do you want, Madame Denavoss?" Eller held his hands up, releasing a slow breath. "We will cooperate. Just... please don't shoot us."

The flashing lights of the bridge danced on Katrielle's grey skin. "I wish not to bring harm to either of you." She jerked her weapon sideways. "Remove your arms slowly and slide them along the floor," she said with a nod.

Sariya reached for her holster.

"*Slowly*," Katrielle reiterated.

Sariya's hand crawled to her belt and pulled out her pistol. She and Eller placed their shock-cannons on the floor and slid them toward Katrielle.

The Imperial woman stepped forward. She kicked away the pistols with her black-and-white high-heel boots. The weapons skipped along, sliding under the circular table at the center of the bridge. The wintry sparkle of her eyes flashed with a mocking enigma.

"Alright. You outplayed us, Kat." Sariya's gloved hands came together for a single fierce clap. "Hiding out in your cabin until you knew our guard was down—very clever of ye, lass. Very clever."

Katrielle nodded once. Her white cloak flickered in the electric light of the transfer cylinders.

"But I don't understand," Sariya said, pointing skyward. "Why not just stay in your cabin, keeping us blissfully ignorant until your Imperial grunts arrived to do your bidding?"

The woman in white's tall, lanky frame inched toward Sariya. "If someone was clever enough to steal my ship while docked at my familial stronghold, they would be clever enough to intercept an encrypted signal transmitting from a vessel in low-power mode." She placed her hand on her hip, speaking through a twisted grin. "I had to get the drop on you while I could." That grin flipped into a sour grimace. "And I had to see it for myself."

"See what?" Sariya asked, her brow rose in feigned girlish innocence.

"You, Sariya Vaeliz. My little cousin... a pirate." She shook her head with a disdainful scoff. "By the Guardians, Sari. Do you realize the plethora of embarrassment and humiliation that you have caused our family? Do you realize how much you have tarnished the Denavoss name?"

"I haven't." Sariya looked to Katrielle with a long blink. "And the idea of it doesn't bother me in the slightest." She leaned back, crossing her hands behind her head.

"I don't believe that, Sariya." Katrielle's cloak flowed behind as she approached her cousin. The aim of her pistol remained stiff. "You are a child of the High Imperium. You are a daughter of the House of Denavoss. This life of a sea thief—it is not for you, regardless of what your father has told—"

"Don't ye bring him into this!" Sariya launched from the seat.

"Whoa, calm yourself!" Katrielle's finger tapped the trigger of her shock-cannon.

"Don't ye blame my father for any of this, *cousin*." Sariya pointed at her in a scolding manner. "Not after everything that ye did to him."

"Easy, Sari." Katrielle's tone turned patronizing. "I do not want to put you down. But I will."

"Sariya," Eller said, leaning toward her. "Take it easy. Sit down."

Sariya let out a sharp sigh and fell back to her seat, her arms crossed tight across her ribs. "Okay. I'm taking it easy." Aggression bled from her words.

Katrielle's aim relaxed. "I am not here to discuss Bellacor Vaeliz. I'm here to make you an offer."

Sariya's head tilted. "You wanna offer *me* something?" She looked to Eller with a squint. "Did she not just catch us making off with her airship?"

As Eller let out a nervous titter, Katrielle continued. "I'm offering you a chance to come home."

For a moment, Sariya stopped breathing. Eller's eyes narrowed.

The Imperial woman looked down on her. "Come home, Sariya. Abandon the life of piracy and pillaging. You *are* Imperial nobility. There is no hiding from it. You may not be entirely Imperial by blood. But you are a gem of the Clerisy, a prize of the promised land."

Sariya scoffed and turned away. "You *can't* be serious, Katrielle."

Katrielle knelt on one knee. "We miss you, Sari. Your *mother* misses you."

"She has never even tried to contact me. She doesn't miss me."

"She absolutely does. She cried for months when you sailed off." Katrielle rested her long, bony hands on Sariya's knee. "She prays for you."

Sariya's head turned toward her cousin with a jolt. "She does?"

"Yes. For safe passage in your journeys at sea. And for you to return home." Her pearly teeth glowed with her smile. "When you're ready."

The young pirate shook her head and rolled her eyes. "She never paid me any mind when I was under her roof. Now she sheds tears for my absence and invokes prayer in my name? How typical."

"Your mother loves you." She took Sariya's hand. "She longs for your return to Sea Haven. And we now have the means to rectify the entire situation."

Sariya gave her cousin a cockeyed stare. "We do?"

Katrielle pointed to Eller. "Say that he made you do it, that you were conscripted into stealing the *Sky Guard* by a cruel pirate."

Eller leaned forward, words on the tip of his tongue.

Katrielle aimed her shock-cannon upon him. "One word and I will discharge this weapon upon your flesh." Her kind eyes wilted to malice. "And my cannon will not be set to incapacitation."

"There's no way that the Clerisy would let me off," Sariya said with a sneer. "They'd still lock me up."

"No, Sariya." Katrielle's long fingernails brushed through Sariya's black hair. "You are a Denavoss. You are nobility. They will give you a mild reprimand and force you to make a public apology. Then you can get back to your life. I know you. You're no pirate. You may have wanted to *perform* as one. But that's not you." She chuckled. "I know how persuasive your father can be. It was *he* who convinced my mother and I to put millions in platinum down for this bloody ship. But he is beneath you, Sariya. You have nothing left to gain from him. Leave him to his eroded ship and his depraved life."

Sariya looked out the window to the shining reflection of the sea. White swirls bathed in moonlight. "I don't know, Kat."

"Come on." Katrielle's fingerless gloves stroked Sariya's face with a delicate caress. "The Imperial Navy will be here soon. We'll speak to them together—as representatives of the Denavoss family. They will bow in reverence to our very presence."

"You know." Sariya looked up at her cousin. "*You* used to like performing as a pirate too, Kat." She spoke through a twisted grin.

"You mean, when you were a child?"

"Aye. When you'd tend to me." Her head tilted back. "We'd run across the harbor, raiding the boats of fishermen and dockworkers, using tiny sticks as swords. And do you remember when our mothers yelled at my father for teaching us seafarer's dialect?"

Katrielle giggled with her cousin. "As well as authentic boarding procedures."

"Aye," Sariya said with a nod. "But ye seem to have forgotten one thing that the captain taught us, Kat."

She leaned forward. "And what is that?"

"When taking a captive, always relieve your opponent of their weapons." Sariya reached for her belt. In a swift motion, she stood and activated her blade. She swung the electrified rapier, and Katrielle's pistol fell to the floor with a sizzle. "Ranged *and* melee."

Katrielle backed away, eyes widened. Sariya approached with caution, her blade held high. The pirate's cousin spun around and sprinted out the door. Her white cloak fluttered in the wind like a ghost in the night.

"Go get her!" Eller ordered, taking hold of the helm with one hand and pointing out the door with the other. "Seize her mobile data system before the Imperium gets here."

"On it!" Sariya reached under the table for her pistol. "I'll incap her and toss her on a lifeboat with the data system. That will throw them off course."

Eller nodded. "I'll put the *Sky Guard* back in the air." His hands gripped the glossy wooden helm. "No point in trying to hide from their tracking now. We need all the speed we can get."

Sariya kicked the door open, sword in one hand and pistol in the other.

"And Sariya," Eller called out, his grip tightening on the joystick. "Hang on tight!" He pulled back, and the *Sky Guard*'s nose tilted upward, rising from the sea surface

The frigid seas sprayed Sariya as the vessel climbed. She leaned against the railing. The *Sky Guard* unleashed a mechanized howl as it accelerated. Salty water dripped down Sariya's face to her lips.

Katrielle stood at a distance. She held on to a chain near the forward electro-sail. Sariya checked to make sure her pistol was set to incapacitate. With one eye shut, she discharged her weapon. One shot was shallow, another wide. The turbulent ascent of the airship rattled her aim. By the time she fired the third, Katrielle had moved out of sight and out of range.

"Damn," she whispered. When the *Sky Guard* leveled, she sprinted across the deck. 'Last thing I need is for her to break for the armory. I have an advantage. I have a pistol. She does not.' Her boots squeaked on the sopping metal of the starboard deck. She held her pistol forward.

A glimpse of white hovered above. As Sariya took aim, a screaming noblewoman plunged from the upper deck. Sariya leapt back, but Katrielle tackled her, prying the shock-cannon from her hands.

The pistol clanked on the floor. Sariya and Katrielle leapt for the weapon and reached the handle simultaneously. Katrielle's hand squeezed the trigger. Sariya pushed the barrel away. Katrielle fired, and a bolt of lightning retreated from the chamber, spiraling into the night sky.

As the electric stream left a trail of thunder, Sariya pushed the pistol away. The two women yanked with all their might. They lost control—and the pistol twirled overboard.

Stepping back, Katrielle drew her broadsword. Her hand wrapped around the thin handle, beneath the curling bars of the sweeping golden hilt. Her thin torso stretched. She pointed the weapon at Sariya. The blade ignited in a hissing flow of voltage. "You don't want to fight me, cousin."

Sariya gave her rapier a twirl. She ignited the blade, its hiss fierce and unsteady compared to the shimmering broadsword held by Katrielle. "Oh, but I do, Madame Denavoss." Her green eyes met her cousin's blue eyes across the luminous fusion of their blades. "I really, really do."

They lunged toward one other, Sariya with a stabbing motion, and Katrielle with a low swipe. Katrielle sidestepped the attack. Sariya leapt and swung down, both hands on her hilt. The Imperial raised her thin blade above her head and stayed the strike.

As Sariya's swing landed, Katrielle pressed her blade into Sariya's, forcing the young pirate off balance. The Imperial utilized her height and reach advantage, pushing Sariya into the taffrail. Her back bending over the edge, Sariya looked down. The *Sky Guard* soared high above sea level. To plummet over the rail would mean her death—she had to escape this position.

In a swift motion, she ducked under her cousin's blade and rolled beside her. Sariya raised her rapier, aiming to strike her opponent's arm with the broad side.

Katrielle twisted with the grace of a dancer and deflected the blade. Her high heels clacked against the deck. She raked her arm right, swiping for Sariya's waist.

Sariya backed away.

Katrielle spun left and unleashed a diagonal slash.

Sariya blocked the attack. But before she could parry, Katrielle raised her sword. Sariya went to thwart the overhead cut—but it was a feint! Katrielle's blade snuck under Sariya's defensive posture. She thrust the broadsword forward. Though Sariya recoiled in evasion, the tip of the sword pierced the inside of her arm.

"Aeeehg!" Sariya screamed at the electric pain. Her left arm fell numb. She recoiled as her cousin advanced in a fluid, disciplined flurry.

"Yield, cousin!" The blue in Katrielle's hair pulsed in the glow of her electric blade. "I have no desire to hurt you."

Sariya felt the wound. 'Mostly cauterized—good,' she thought.

"Nor I, you, Kat!" Sariya stood tall with a slanted smile. "So, yield the data system that is putting out the distress beacon. And we can call it a day."

"You will always be a Denavoss in my eyes, Sariya."

She sprinted forward and swung her sword across her body. Sariya raised her rapier to block the strike. Their eyes met over their clashing blades. Sparks emitted.

Katrielle's voice growled under the scorching hiss. "But you will *never* take my ship."

"It's not your ship!" Sariya kicked Katrielle in the stomach.

The Imperial fell back with a gasp, but the kick passed through her. She found her balance and assumed a defensive stance. "Sariya, you know that's not proper swordsmanship."

"Who gives a damn?" Sariya said with a smirk. "All that matters is that it got me this." She held up a thin, square data system in her right hand. The pirate had snatched it from Katrielle's pocket while their blades met.

"No!" Katrielle yelled.

Sariya tossed it overboard.

The winds whistled over the droning electro-sail. Sariya looked to her cousin with a smile. "Let us negotiate your surrender."

Katrielle looked down on Sariya with a pompous raise of her chin. "I don't think so," she said with a scornful tone. That is when Sariya noticed a blinking device above her gold earring: a communication system, no doubt feeding her cousin's location to the knights at Seas Haven Castle

"Ugh, by the Guardians. It never ends." Sariya stepped forward in a series of cross-body slashes. Katrielle blocked them with ease.

Their duel continued across the *Sky Guard*. The steam of their breath swirled around their clashing blades. The black in Sariya's hair fluttered opposite the pale blonde of Katrielle's.

Katrielle backed Sariya up the stairs, to the top deck by the main cannon. There had to be an opening—a weakness in her form. But Sariya could not find it. Every time she counterattacked, Katrielle parried. 'It's like she knows what I am going to do before I do it.'

Sariya slid forward in a string of one-handed cuts. Her cousin evaded the attacks and forced Sariya back with an aggressive onslaught.

As she lost her footing, she studied her cousin's stance. It was formulaic—a series of sequential movements designed to dispel cavalier dueling styles like Sariya's. As she blocked the strikes, she memorized Katrielle's movements. Spin, low swipe, feign cross-slash into a thrust, parry into a flourishing twist. 'How do I get in?' Sariya thought. 'I have to do something she doesn't expect—which means I have to do something that *I* don't expect."

Sariya broke from the duel and ran to the other side of the cannon. Katrielle chased her. As she came around the turret, Sariya grabbed hold of the barrel. When Katrielle followed, Sariya rode her momentum and released her grip from the long bar. She soared forward and kicked her cousin's ribs.

Katrielle slid down the side of the cannon to the deck below. Sariya vaulted after her. With her opponent on her back, Sariya swung her blade downward. Katrielle raised the broadsword high above with a clenched snarl.

Their blades connected once more. As Katrielle moved to stand, Sariya stomped on her cousin's stomach. The Imperial woman's grip loosened, and Sariya's fingers wrapped around the swirled hilt of the broadsword.

With a cough, Katrielle dragged herself backward. Sariya stood over her cousin with a wide stance and crossed the blades over her torso, their electric streams fizzling against one another. "Take out the communication device," Sariya demanded.

"No!"

"I said take... it... out." She held the crossed blades over her cousin's neck.

Katrielle's shoulders slumped. She removed the small black device from the inside of her ear.

"Deactivate it."

With a touch of Katrielle's finger, the device beeped and shut itself off. "You do know that you have lost, right? This girlish pretense matters not. You lost." Her head tilted. An arrogant smile bled from her smeared platinum lipstick. "Even without a tracking device, do you think you can hide from the might of the High Imperium?" A mocking chuckle interrupted her words. "Even if you make it out of Imperial waters and keep her seabound to confuse our satellites, you'll never hide the *Sky Guard* from us. She is too large." With a slow shake of her head, her words seeped like poison. "And to think that I offered you a chance to return to a beautiful life in Sea Haven."

Sariya responded with a tight grin. "Hiding her was never my plan, Katrielle. But Rogue Haven law does factor in."

"What are you talking about?"

"Rogue Haven practices the Law of Shipwright's Claim. My father never signed ownership of his vessel to you. In Rogue Haven, the law would recognize the *Sky Guard* as his."

Katrielle broke into laughter. Sariya pulled the swords back to avoid burning her chin. "You really think that kind of nonsense would hold up in court? Your negligent father may have drawn the plans for the *Sky Guard*. But he never owned this vessel. He abandoned his duties before he saw the work completed."

Sariya shrugged. "True. Maybe it wouldn't hold up in Imperial court. But it would in Rogue Haven. It is my father who is treated as nobility in the Vanden Reaches. Not you, Katrielle."

Katrielle shivered. It was strange to see an Imperial shiver. "Nobility," she said through rattling teeth. "He is a pirate. A low-life smuggler. A common thief—

"An industrious contractor, a gallant mercenary, a beloved employer of more than a hundred and twenty lads and lasses." She smiled, looking down at her older cousin. "You see, Kat. In the Reaches, my father's a respected man. That'd be why he felt no need to take any more disparagement from the likes of you and me mother."

She leaned back with a sneer. Sariya was mindful of her cousin's movements, but she remained resigned. "Regardless of your father's status as *folk hero*, I have the Imperial Navy at my call," Katrielle said. "They will dispatch of you both with ease."

"The Imperial Navy has no jurisdiction in Vanden waters."

"Jurisdiction will have nothing to do with it when they sink you."

Sariya's head tilted. Her bandana let a strand of hair fall loose over her face. "Kat, the Imperium is not permitted to engage in any sort of militaristic exercise in the Vanden Reaches without Vandeni consent. Something tells me that your favoritism with the Clerisy stops short of an act of war."

"Little cousin." Katrielle's eyes burned like the bottom of a flame. "No one will know that the Imperium sank your ships. When they find your bodies, they will simply assume that you and your illicit father died in a pirate skirmish on the open sea. Such a *tragic* waste of life."

A silence fell between the two women. The clouds churned by, and the stars shined through. "Or instead of sinking your own ship, you could keep it as an asset. Just in a different respect."

"What are you talking about?"

Sariya twirled one of the swords, a grin sliding up the side of her face. "Charter my father's fleet for your service: the *Sky Guard*, the *Ocean Flame*. When there is something that ye need done—sensitive matters which require both discretion and enforcement—we'll take care of it. And at a discounted family rate."

Katrielle sat silently, her jaw dropping.

"This is more ship than ye know what to do with, cousin." Sariya gestured to the large turrets. "The *Sky Guard* was built for more than banquets and wine tastings." She aimed one of the electro-blades toward the summit. "I presume that there are certain... jobs that you and the rest of the Denavoss household would like done. Jobs that you can't do yourself. That's where we come in."

Katrielle squinted and looked down. "That is the most *absurd* and *offensive* suggestion that I have ever heard. You may as well just kill me now. I would never agree to something so preposterous."

"Killing you would give me neither profit nor pleasure, Kat," Sariya said. "I don't expect you to make a decision right now. Think about it for a while. Maybe you decide that it's in your best interest—in your family's best interest. Or perhaps you'll decide to leave it be and cut your losses—let my father and I have the *Sky Guard*, as it is rightfully ours."

Katrielle shook her head and lifted her chin.

"You were right, Katrielle." Sariya knelt and placed a hand on Katrielle's shoulder, holding the electro-blade away from her body. "I *do* want a place in the House of Denavoss. I *do* want to have my mother, Aunt Aritha, and you in my life. But it has to be on *my* terms."

The woman in white's stare was blank, dead and wrathful.

"But let me make one thing perfectly clear to ye, Katrielle." Sariya leaned close. Her face hovered over her cousin's. "If you do launch an attack on me and my father, ye might win. Ye may get what you desire: my body forever drowning in the fathoms." Her voice trembled. "But if we win the battle, I will bring together the seafolk of Vanda in an armada that the world hasn't seen since the War of Empires. I will launch a large-scale assault on Sea Haven Castle. I will pound every stone with artillery until it is indistinguishable from the rubble that it was built from."

Katrielle shook her head. "By the mercy of the Guardians, you would destroy our familial home?"

"Only if you destroy my father's."

Sariya Vaeliz walked Katrielle Denavoss to the ancillary craft. Katrielle asked for her sword back. Sariya refused but did return her communication system. "I do look forward to our next meeting, cousin," Sariya said as Katrielle entered the craft.

Katrielle did not answer.

Sariya added, "Whatever the nature of our encounter may be."

"As do I," Katrielle uttered.

The hatch shut, and the ancillary craft plummeted from the *Sky Guard*. A small electrical thruster slowed the boat's descent as it fell toward the sea.

Sariya prayed that a rescue team would recover her soon.

"Hey, Sariya!" Eller's voice came into her ear. "We're passing into the Syrenian Sea! We're in neutral waters!"

Sariya made her way back to the bridge.

VII. A Sizable Plunder

Throughout the journey, Sariya and Eller traded control of the helm for the twin-sized bed that pulled out from the floor.

Eller did not rest easy. "Keep her steady!" he would yell, bursting from his slumber. "You keep over-anticipating your turns. You're going to catch us in turbulence."

"Apologies," Sariya would say with a nod.

As Athenis rose, Sariya sent an encoded message—a signal only known to the *Ocean Flame*. For quite some time, there was no reply.

Finally, an answer came from Paksly in communication.

Sariya's face hung over the terminal. "We're crossing through the Vanden Reaches." Paksly transmitted the *Ocean Flame*'s coordinates. "We'll hold our position until your arrival," she said.

"You... didn't tell them we'd be arriving in the *Sky Guard*." Eller's voice was cracked and groggy.

"I know," Sariya said. "I want to surprise them!"

"That's great. So long as they don't shoot us down."

Four hours later, the *Sky Guard* approached the *Ocean Flame*. Sariya sent a message. "This is Sailor Sariya Vaeliz reporting with Third Officer Eller Oravessi. We are approaching now and preparing to make contact."

"Copy that," a voice replied. "But all I see on the scopes is an airship, matey. Is that...? Oh, by the rage of the sea, she actually did it."

With Eller at the helm, Sariya ran out to the nose of the *Sky Guard*. The airship slowed. As it thundered past the *Ocean Flame*, the crew packed themselves on the top deck. Sariya raised her fist in the air. Over the hiss of the ships' electro-sails, the crew roared with cheer. At least, some of them.

She saluted the *Ocean Flame*, leaning over the taffrail.

"Mind helping me land?" Eller asked via communication system.

"Of course not."

After the *Sky Guard* descended into the water, Eller and Sariya held her position by the *Ocean Flame*. The celebrating sailors aboard her father's ship cheered louder yet. Thraeliss and Dorgallik tossed a chain over the gap between the two ships. Sariya grabbed hold and swung across. Before making her landing, she was surrounded by congratulatory pats on the back. Sariya tossed the chain back so that Eller could join her.

"The adventuresome swashbuckler returns!" Dorkallik shouted, his fishy breath invading Sariya's nose.

Thraeliss looked to her with a serpentine smile. "Forget everything I said. You're no princess of the Imperium. Sariya, you're a queen of the sea!"

"Ow!" Sariya said as Thraeliss' sharp claws squeezed her shoulder.

"Oh, sorry."

Sariya beamed with a grin, waving off her apology. Mylia, Sariya's roommate, barreled through the crowd and gave her a forceful kiss on the forehead. Sariya's eyes swiveled back and forth.

"You're a genius!" Mylia shouted. "Look at her—look at that monstrous beauty." Mylia's jaw dropped to reveal yellowed teeth as she approached the *Sky Guard*.

Ithia from navigation embraced Sariya in a warm hug. "I knew you could do it, lil' lassie."

"Thanks, Ithia," Sariya whispered under the sound of cheer.

"Vaeliz!" Halsik's gruff voice yelled. The sailors cleared a path for their second officer. "I've been humbled. You did something right. Once." He extended his hand. Sariya's palm crossed his, and they exchanged a firm shake. He pulled her close and whispered, "Don't ye dare get to thinking this little stunt will put your standing above mine." His grip constricted Sariya's hand as he trapped the young girl in a narrow gaze. "First mate is *still* mine."

She smiled and uttered in his ear, "No need to feel humbled, Officer Halsik." Her voice was soft, while sharp, like velvet and rose thorns. "If it wasn't for you, I'd never have had the spine to go through with it." She motioned to the celebrating members of the crew. "Do you really want to run against me when my presence is sparking such enthusiasm?"

The sweaty, bearded man growled in her ear. "You will *not* have first officer."

"We can both have it."

"What are you yabbering about?"

Sariya chuckled. "You're going to put me up for the vote for first officer of the *Ocean Flame*."

"You must be drunker than a seagull in saloon trash—"

"And I'll put *you* up for the *Sky Guard*."

He slumped and froze, looking to the mighty airship.

She straightened and raised her voice. "Deal?"

He snarled and nodded, peeling his eyes away from the new vessel for but a moment. "Deal."

Eller swung across on the chain. Sariya stepped away from Halsik. She stood high and shouted, "Mates of the *Ocean Flame*!" The celebrating men and women quieted down—enough to hear her, anyway. "I am proud to have commandeered the mighty *Sky Guard*. But your humble Third Officer, Eller Oravessi, was the true hero of the escapade!"

Before Sariya could finish, the howls of the crew intensified. They rushed to the side of the deck and hailed Eller with the same enthusiasm. "Eller! Eller! Eller!" they chanted as Dorgallik lifted him to his shoulders.

Thraeliss approached Sariya like a wild predator.

"No, no!" Sariya said with a nervous laugh.

But Thraeliss lifted her above the crowd of men and women. From the Draekalagon's shoulders, she saw that not everyone was cheering or even content. Those not surrounding Sariya and Eller to sing their praises stood slumped with their arms crossed, biting their nails, exchanging skeptical glances.

Over the horde, Sariya looked to Eller with a slight shrug.

"Sailor Vaeliz!" The cheers and chants fell silent under the calm swirl of the sea. Captain Bellacor Vaeliz stood at the stern, donning a black leather coat and a matching tricorn hat. "Come hither, young lass."

Thraeliss let her down. The crowd parted as Sariya stepped up the grated staircase. "Yes, Captain?" she asked with her hands behind her back, standing at attention.

"Do you mean to tell me that you defied my direct orders...?" Captain Bellacor took a long step forward. His blank blue face drowned in Athenis' early noon glow. "That you seized one of my attack boats, made for Sea Haven in the middle of the night? That you broke into your mother's castle and stole the *Sky Guard* from your dear cousin? And that you recklessly flew it back with only two of ye—when that ship is designed to be crewed by a minimum of forty?" He pointed to the *Sky Guard*. The airship stretched past and towered over the *Ocean Flame*.

"Correct, Captain," Sariya said with a nod.

Bellacor smiled and leaned over the railing. "What ye think, lads? Is she a daughter of mine or what?"

"Yeah!" was the consensus of much of the crew.

Halsik rushed up the stairs. "Captain!" he said, a sinister smile beneath his bushy black beard.

"Yes, Officer Halsik?"

"I'd like to put forward a vote to the crew."

The captain nodded. "Speak your piece, mate."

Halsik shouted. "I hereby nominate Sariya Vaeliz for first mate of the *Ocean Flame*!"

The air escaped Sariya's lungs. He actually did it. Tears flooded her eyes faster than she thought was possible.

Dozens of men and women replied with an aggressive, "Aye!" Others looked to each other in confusion, wanting to see how their contemporaries voted before casting one themselves. But when they saw the grisly stare of Halsik peeling them apart from the quarterdeck, more "Ayes" burst from the sailors like dominos falling in neat rows.

Sariya turned away, hiding her face. Halsik rested his hand on her back. "Sariya Vaeliz!" he shouted.

"First mate!" the chorus of the crew replied.

"Sariya Vaeliz!"

"First mate!"

"Well, that settles it, then." Captain Bellacor's steps thumped on the metal deck. "My daughter as my own first mate." He wiped her tears away. "And ye earned it, like you said you would."

Sariya smiled and turned around. Halsik watched her with earnest anticipation. "Sailors of the *Ocean Flame*!" she shouted. They quieted once more. "I put forth my first vote as first mate of the *Ocean Flame*! Officer Halsik served as an officer on a cargo barge: an airship."

Halsik nodded and looked to the crew with a grin. "When I was younger and slimmer," his burly voice bellowed.

Sariya smiled. "My dear lads and lasses, I nominate Zanen Halsik as first officer of the *Sky Guard*!"

"Yeah!" was the response, this time nearly unanimous.

"So long as you'll approve this nomination, Captain?" She looked over her shoulder at her father.

"Aye," Captain Bellacor said with a nod. He looked to Halsik. "First Mate Halsik, start rounding up a crew for the *Sky Guard*. Engineers, navigators, maintenance workers. Preferably those who have experience on airships like yerself."

"Aye, sir!" he replied before scurrying down the stairs.

"Wait!" one of the crew in the back shouted. "That leaves an opening at the *Ocean Flame*'s second mate position."

"Let us be led by the commandeering duo!" Thraeliss yelled.

"Eller!" a woman shouted.

"Second mate!" replied the crew.

"Eller!"

"Second mate!"

Captain Bellacor shrugged, his hands on the railing, overlooking his men and women. "I guess the ranks are changing dramatically today."

The crew, gathered near quarterdeck, laughed with their leader. The sailors in the middle of the deck seemed less amused, even those who had reluctantly voted for Sariya Vaeliz as first mate of the *Ocean Flame*. Near the front of the ship, below the forecastle deck, Eldofain, the Imperial lookout, trapped her in a stare of uncouth disgust. A host of crewmen behind him mimicked his demeanor.

Captain Bellacor turned to Sariya and put his hand on her shoulder. "Well lass, this is a... rather sizable plunder that you brought us." He looked upon the *Sky Guard*. "When I heard that Katrielle had continued production without my consent, I never thought that I'd see her with my own eyes. I thought blueprints was the closest I would get."

"Now she's yours, Captain," Sariya said with a bow of her head.

"She's ours," the captain replied. He gestured to the ship with a boisterous stride. "She's ours, lads. She's ours!"

The crew chanted. "*Sky Guard! Sky Guard! Sky Guard!*"

"I'm going to go take a look at her with a few of the sailors," the captain said. He looked to Sariya and Eller with a smile. "Think the two of ye can keep them in check until I get back?" His eyes crawled to the excitable men and women below.

"I think we can manage, can't we, Sariya?" Eller asked.

"Aye!" she replied.

"Good work, the two of ye." He looked at the *Sky Guard* with a sigh. "We're gunna have to rip out her navigation system and any ID codes in her central data core. We can't have anything that Katrielle can track. When we get to Rogue Haven, we'll alter the architectural details and reshape her hull. We can make her look like an entirely different ship."

"Father, don't worry about any of that," Sariya said. "I don't think Katrielle is going to be a problem."

He squinted. "Did you have an encounter with your cousin? What deal did ye strike?"

"I'll explain later. For now, go explore your ship. She's waiting for ye."

"I do long to walk her halls," Bellacor said with a nod. He wrapped his daughter in a tight hug. "But don't ever scare me like that again, Sariya Vaeliz. I love you."

"Love ye, Cap."

She wiped her tears as her father walked away. He took hold of the chain and swung across to the *Sky Guard*. Raising a fist in the air once his feet touched the deck, he signaled for the rest of the party to follow.

"By the life light of Athenis," Eller said, crossing his arms. "Did we really just do that? Or is this some kind of odd dream that will make even less sense when I wake up?"

Sariya smiled and tapped him on the elbow. "El, I couldn't have done it without ye. None of it."

Eller looked her way. "Be honest with me, Sariya. Was tricking me into coming along really part of your plan?"

She shook her head. "Not exactly. I didn't have much of a plan at all. But when you caught me on the deck, I knew I needed to have ye by my side. If I didn't, I'd be rotting in a dungeon or washing my cousin's linens by now." She reached across his back and rested her head on his shoulder. "So, thank ye, mate. Thank ye for everything."

Eller grabbed hold of her hand and squeezed tight. "Think we can get these sailors in line?"

Sariya peered up, her green eyes beaming with her smile. "Hopefully they can keep up."

"Everyone back to work!" Eller shouted. The voices of the crew settled.

"That's right, ye reef-driftin' bottom feeders. Get back to yer tasks. The celebration's over."

Eller screamed to a group of sailors. "The seas are calm, but it may not stay that way for long. You know how swift the winds can change in these waters. Run a maintenance check on the weather equipment."

Sariya pointed to Thraeliss. "Sailor Thraeliss, the captain took several of the maintenance crew with him. Why don't you see if our remaining workers on the *Flame* could use an extra hand?"

"Aye, matey!" Thraeliss replied.

Eller took hold of the wheel. "Navigation team, prepare to set course for Rogue Haven."

"You okay to take the helm?" she asked. "You've been up at the wheel most of the night already."

"I'm wide awake."

"Me too!" Sariya eyed the lookout tower. "I'm going up to the nest. Easier to keep an eye on these scruffy chaps from up there."

Eller nodded. "Aye!"

Sariya ran toward the metal ladder and hopped on. "Avast, mateys! I see ye skulking about. We ain't got no time for wake drifting. We're undermanned. So, find the fire of your souls that keeps the *Flame* afloat. When we get to Rogue Haven, whisky, ale and mindless indulgence will wash the pains of our labor away!"

"Aye!" the crew replied.

"Make sure that our artillery is primed!" Eller shouted, turning the wheel away from the airship. "The *Sky Guard* is bound to attract jealous eyes. We must be prepared to defend her."

Sariya climbed higher, hanging off the ladder with one hand. "And I want the electro-sail in peak condition. The *Ocean Flame* needs to be ready to set out as soon as the captain and First Mate Halsik give the signal."

She reached the top of the lookout tower.

"First Officer Sariya!" Eller yelled from below.

"Aye?" She peered over the edge of the platform.

"Perhaps you ought to lead these chaps in a shanty." He looked up with a smile. "Fill their spirits with unity and workmanship."

"I think you're right, matey!" Sariya leaned over the railing. Athenis gleamed in the swelling mirror of the sea. She looked south toward the horizon. With a deep breath, she tasted the fresh, briny air.

She began to sing, or melodically shout, so the sailors could hear her below. *"I hear the fair maiden's call on the distant island shore."*

The crew responded in unison, Eller's voice singing the top harmony. *"The lads and lasses beg of me: bring her on aboard."*

Sariya chanted the next line. *"But I can't, ye see, as they ask of me. Me mates don't know I'm torn."*

And the crew replied again. *"Though my heart does fall with the maiden's call, it's the sea which I love more."*

THE RIDER IN BLACK

The rider in black rode across the desert plains, fleeing from the crushing darkness of the starless sky. Unable to distinguish the thumping of her heart from the violent gallop of her reptilian mount, she carried on through the night. The cacti closed in, a desert forest. Their crooked arms reached forward in an offer of penetrating embrace. Travel lights would help, but the rider dared not activate them. If she did, they would see. If they saw, they would follow. If they followed, they would catch her. If they caught her...

'No, they won't catch me,' she thought. 'I'll die first.'

Her trugan, the reptilian beast on which she rode, released a guttural cry. She was tired. She was in pain.

"No!" shouted the young woman. "We have to keep going. They're behind us."

Another cry from the mount.

"Stop it, Kaiar!" The woman kicked the beast and slapped down the reins. "We have to keep moving. We have to keep moving."

The creature's forked tongue drooped over her scaly jaw. The cybernetic systems beneath her skin moaned at a high pitch, under heavy stress. Kaiar was moving at maximum speed, and the rider in black knew this, yet she kicked her mount again.

"Go!"

The cacti grew nearer, leaned lower, reached closer. Shadows painted maniacal, laughing faces on their indigo trunks. Kaiar zigzagged around the encroaching plant life. The woman held her pistol tight and turned around, for she was certain that they followed, that the Red River Gang followed. She swore she heard the stampeding gallop of their trugan. But there was no one there, at least no one that she could see. If only she had an optical system with night-vision capability; if only she had a sniper rifle; if only she could rest for a moment.

It was not too much longer to Blood Boulder Basin. She could stop in the inn for the night and... no. No, that would not do. They could be waiting. They *would* be waiting. Half of Blood Boulder Basin's Marshal's Department was on their payroll. Their crooked badges would reveal her whereabouts! Her captors would break down her door at the inn. With any luck, they would shoot her on sight. But they would not let her down so easy, they would not grant the luxury of a swift death.

'I will not be your slave,' she thought. 'I will not take another life. I won't do it. Never again. Never again.' She clenched her fist and winced, unsure whether the cold liquid between her fingers was sweat or blood. 'Never... again.'

The clouds swirled in thick clusters, threatening rainfall. Darkness loomed. The cacti's silhouettes faded from view. A descending mist hid the expanse of the desert, taking the form of dying faces in dreadful agony. Ghosts in the night begging for aid, for mercy, for a chance to make amends.

Kai struggled to keep pace. The rider slapped the reins upon her neck, but the beast was no longer able to heed the command. She slowed more and more yet. The rider prepared to give Kaiar a stern kick, when she looked up and realized that she had lost her bearings. The fog had shrouded her path and confused her sense of direction; she rode through a wide gorge that she did not recognize. How far had she ridden past Blood Boulder Basin? Which direction had she gone? Had she accidentally turned around? Was she riding right back into the clutches of her captors? She had to stop. Not just for her own sake, but for Kaiar's. If she made the beast ride at high speeds any longer, her bionic organs would cease to function and they would be stranded in the desert, in the middle of nowhere, possibly hundreds of miles away from any semblance of civilization.

The rider in black dismounted. Immediately, Kaiar fell to the ground, sending heavy vibrations through the sandy terrain. The rider then realized how exhausted *she* was. Each heavy breath brought great pain to her bruised ribs. Making camp was not an option. While she did not know where she was, they could follow her tracks. Stopping was a terrible idea to begin with. But she had to get her bearings somehow. The stars still failed to pierce the veil of mist and clouds, thus could not serve as a guide. The moons were new, their shape hidden from the eyes of the world. She did not have a data system to help chart the way. She had not dared bring any equipment provided by her captors, for they placed trackers on their expensive gear.

"Where are we, Kai?"

The beast had no answer. Her forked tongue dangled from the side of her mouth as she panted into the desert sands. The rider went to fetch some water from the pannier atop the beast's saddle—and heard a sound. Something watched. Something approached. Something circled. The danger was all in her head; it had to be in her head, as many of the night's terrors had been. It was nothing. It had to be nothing. Just a feeling. As she reached down to pick up her canteen, Kaiar stopped panting and turned her head up. The beast's vertical pupils narrowed to thin slits. She hissed, growled and began to sniff, turning her head, tracking something.

This was no imaginary threat. "What is it?" the rider in black whispered. "What do you see? What do you smell?" Kaiar's knees shook as she came to her feet. The rider turned around and drew her pistol. Were they here? Had they caught up?

"Who's there?" the rider called out. Her voice echoed dozens of times off the walls of the gorge, but there was no response. She took aim with her pistol and drew her electro-blade. She had to know what was out there, stalking her through the mist in the barren lands of this nameless gorge. She ignited the electrical current of her blade even at risk of compromising her position. Flashes of purple and white ignited around the weapon, and the electric layer cast an aura of visibility around its shape. That aura revealed the hungry eyes of a great beast standing less than a yard from the rider in black. Its red eyes flashed in the electric glow. Its long, sharp teeth protruded in front of its chin as its angry face vibrated with a snarl. The rider gasped and froze before the grey-furred beast pounced with claws extended.

Instinctively, the young woman raised her blade to defend herself. But the beast leapt over the rider, for she was not the target. Kaiar was. The saddled reptile fought back with her fangs, but the wild mammal clasped its jaws around her neck. Gnashing and twisting its head, the cougar forced Kaiar down to the sands. Despite the trugan's size and strength advantage, the nimble cat was able to exploit Kaiar's depleted body. The trugan clawed and bit back, thrusting her horn forward to protect her vulnerable throat. She tried to regain her footing to better defend herself, but the cougar kept her pinned, attempting to stab its long canines into the reptile's jugular. Even Kaiar's bionic organs could not save her.

"No!" yelled the rider in black. She charged toward the massive battling animals, electro-sword held before her. 'No one else is dying because of me.' She lunged forward and singed the cougar's hip with the tip of the blade. The beast yelped and released her clasp on Kaiar's neck but remained atop her. The woman attacked again in a repeated series of swipes and stabs, careful to make contact only with the cougar and not with her trugan. The cougar would not relent. It persisted in its attempt to sink its dagger-like fangs into Kaiar's neck. The rider took aim with her pistol. She did not trust herself to fire, for the trugan and the cougar twisted each other through the sands in combat. If she hit Kaiar, even with her pistol in low-power mode, she could stop her heart while she was in this weak, wounded and exhausted state.

So the woman fired her weapon into the air. The startled wild creature looked to the heavens at the thunderous blast of electricity rocketing toward the clouds. She caught the cat off guard and lunged again with her electro-sword. The beast noticed her a moment too late, and she was able to get a strong swipe across the top of its chest. With a yelp of pain, the saber-tooth leapt off Kaiar and rolled in the dirt to douse the orange embers on its grey fur.

The beast came to its feet, and its red eyes burned with vengeful fury. It circled again, not Kaiar this time, but the rider in black. The rider raised her sword, putting herself between the snarling cat and her reptilian mount. Kaiar attempted to stand, though her wobbling knees would not allow it.

"I got this," said the rider. "Stay back, Kai. I got this one."

With a reluctant groan, the saddled reptile collapsed again. The rider looked to the cougar. "Come on!" she yelled with a twist of her electric weapon. "You want her, you're going to have to go through me." The cougar's pupils narrowed, and it knelt low, preparing to pounce. "Come on!" yelled the rider again.

The beast gave in to provocation and launched itself toward the young woman. The woman gasped and rolled to the side to avoid its monstrous claws. While she was crouched, the cougar went to strike again, this time with a bite. But the rider brought her blade forward and kept the wild predator back. Its eyes turned to crimson flame in the electric glow of the weapon. Backing away, it circled again. The cat's head tilted back and forth as if it were in thought. The woman reached for her pistol and took aim, but the beast thrust its mighty paw into the terrain and launched a bombardment of sand into her eyes.

The woman backed away with a groan, attempting to flush the grains of the desert with rapid blinking. Before she could raise her blade, the cougar pounced. She raised her arm in time to keep her blade before her, but the beast pinned her shoulders with its paws and brought her to the ground.

The clever little desert hunter had figured out that the only thing between itself and its prey was a weak Vandeni woman with modern weaponry. And it had figured out how to take that modern weaponry away.

'Got to admit,' thought the rider as she struggled to keep the blade between herself and the beast, 'you outsmarted me there.'

The saber-toothed cougar's hot breath rained on her face as it leaned closer and opened its jaws wider. The rider in black struggled to thrust her sword forward, hoping to singe the beast once more and break its hold on her. But it was no use; the creature had figured out how to eliminate the blade as a threat. It was going to stab its fangs into the rider's neck.

But the beast yelped and jolted back when Kaiar, enraged and feral, sank her teeth deep into the large cat's hip. While the cougar struggled to break free, the woman escaped and took aim with her pistol.

"Kai, move!"

Kaiar did as instructed. The woman fired two shots from her shock-cannon, rendering the saber-tooth unconscious, the shots' thunderous echoes ringing off the walls of the gorge. As her heartbeat shook her chest, she caught her breath and looked to the incapacitated mammal. Smoke rose from its fur as its body twitched. Its eyes fluttered in an uneasy rest. The woman's black-gloved hand shook as she kept aim on the wild beast. Her finger began to squeeze the trigger—then, she bit her lip and holstered her pistol with a strained moan. Her attention turned to Kaiar. The trugan had several bite wounds just below her neck, where her hide was soft and tender.

"Kai," whimpered the woman. "Kai, I'm so sorry."

The beast groaned and limped to its rider. She held her head low and nuzzled her snout into the woman's torso.

"I rode you too hard. I should have listened to you. I'm so, so sorry." Kai had several scratch marks along her back and going down her left flank. "Come on," said the woman, pulling on her reins. "We have to keep moving on foot. We need to get you to a veterinarian and a cybernetics engineer. And you're not strong enough to bear me as a burden right now."

They walked past the saber-tooth cougar one last time. Kaiar presented the unconscious beast with a final hiss of warning, just in case it would
dare to awaken. The rider gave the desert predator a nod.

They traversed the gorge on a path that never seemed to diverge or
end. Somehow, the idea that her captors would catch up no longer felt
like an imminent risk. The rider and her steed would be lost forever in
this hazy darkness. No one would be able to find their way in or out,
including them. The rider was tired. She was hungry. Kaiar was wounded
and overworked beyond her natural or automated capabilities. In this
fog they would be lost forever, watched by the curious yellow eyes of the
desert owls as they slowly turned to bone.

In this gorge, they were in the mouth of the wilderness. And this
wilderness was not only unforgiving, but forever hungry, forever de-
manding of a respect that the rider was in no position to offer. She was
unprepared to cross the remote plains of Vanda. In this desert, lack of
preparation was a sin, a sin that many had perished from for commit-
ting. How many lay dead under the sands after taking a fall from their
trugan, from consuming a wild nectar full of dangerous toxins, from a
wild animal attack, from starvation, thirst, exhaustion? The wilds were
a graveyard for the unwary, and soon the rider would join them.

'Very soon,' she thought as she swirled her canteen. She dared not take
a sip. Her thirst was overwhelming in the dark. In a few hours, at Athenis'
rise, her thirst would consume her.

For hours, they wandered the gorge. The woman in black fell into
a trance. She had learned to become content with the silent darkness,
with the imminence of death. The terrain rose in a series of dunes, each
higher than the last. At the end of the final dune, the heavy fog began to
dissipate. On the eastern horizon, a shard of blue pierced the sky. Athenis
was on the rise. Relief came to the woman, as she knew the darkness

would soon be a memory, a nightmare that her mind would suppress. But her knees were weak, her throat was dry and her breath was heavy. She could not go on much longer. The desert heat would be swift to claim her soul.

Kaiar approached from the rear and nudged the rider in the arm.

"You want some water, girl?"

The trugan turned her head to the side, making a motion toward her saddle.

"Kai, no. You can't take me on your back right now. You're too weak."

The beast grunted and nudged her again.

"But... but you could die."

Kaiar knelt low and bowed her head.

"I guess we're dead if we don't get a move on anyway, huh?"

The rider was careful to avoid her trugan's wounds when she sat atop the saddle. The draconic beast groaned as she came back to her feet, her knees shaking, her bones cracking. As she built up speed, the rider in black cast anything off the pannier that they did not need: camping supplies, tools, emergency equipment. Anything to lighten the load of her wounded companion.

With aid from her malfunctioning cybernetics, Kaiar was able to carry on at a faster speed than natural for a trugan, though she was nowhere near her top speed. The rider did not direct her mount in any particular direction. She trusted that Kaiar somehow knew the way, somehow had an idea of how to rescue them from the deathly blue heat of Athenis, from the circling vultures above, from the silver fang snake coiled around the closest indigo cactus. Wait, was there a silver fang around that cactus? No, it could not have been. They only lived in deep southern Vanda, where there was less competition for prey. What would a silver fang be doing in the middle of the continent? If she was still *in* the middle of the continent.

'I am losing my mind.'

After traversing a barren stretch of hardpan, Kaiar made a sharp left turn. In the distance, the rider saw a sign. Perhaps it was a hallucination, but it was worth investigating to find out for sure. She directed Kaiar toward the old wooden board ahead. The beast labored across the harsh terrain, where nothing grew, and nothing lived. Even gravel seemed to avoid the area. The crooked signpost sat lonely in the ground, and the rider finally got close enough to read the faded black paint. "Stormgate: 12 miles."

"We're almost there, girl. We're almost there."

The burning rays of aridity reached into the hunter's throat as if strangling her from within. Her head throbbed and pulsed. She felt imbalanced, woozy, mangled. She thought she may collapse until she saw an assemblage of wooden structures in the distance. Another mirage. It must be. And she refused to believe otherwise until she crossed the border of the town to the smell of sawdust and the rhythmic beating of a blacksmith's hammer. Suspicious citizens looked on from the wooden walkways. An opposing group of riders on truganback stared before giving an awkward greeting, their heads remaining cocked toward the woman in black as they passed.

'Why are they looking at me like that?' she asked herself. 'Do I really look that out of place, that strange, that foreign? What am I doing wrong? I can't attract too much attention.'

With that thought, she remembered. She remembered why she had run in the first place. She remembered the pursuit of her captors. She remembered the horrible fate that she would meet if they did find her.

She remembered the deathly anguish in his screams, the screams of the man who she once considered a friend as he called her name...

"A veterinarian," she whispered, interrupting her own panicked thoughts. "I need a vet for Kai. She's about to collapse."

She found a veterinarian near the end of town. The white-bearded old man stated that he could treat Kaiar's wounds from the saber-tooth attack and give her some medication to help her vitals normalize after such strenuous riding. But he could not do anything to repair her bionic organs, for he had no expertise in cybernetics, nor did anyone in the town of Stormgate.

"That's fine," said the rider. "I can take her to an expert in the next town. Just get her in the best shape you can."

He looked the emerald-scaled beast up and down. "You rode her into the ground pretty hard, there."

The rider swallowed and turned her head. "She can handle it."

He stepped forward, looking down on her through his long white lashes. "What are you running from, kid?"

"Forty platinum, right?"

"Well yes, but..."

"Here's fifty." The young woman stepped out of the vet's stable before he could get another word in. She turned the corner as Kaiar called to her with a high-pitched moan. "I'll be back, girl," she said, her voice shaking. "I'll be back. Don't worry. He'll take good care of you."

Stormgate did not have an inn but a boarding house. She made her way to the tall wooden structure with an angular roof that stood down the street from the veterinarian's facility. The dull coat of blue paint gave the building a more welcoming aura than the rest of the town had. She stepped through the doors to enter a narrow hallway with white rocking chairs on either side.

A woman wearing a red dress with floral patterns stepped out from the kitchen. "Hello there," she said with a cheerful smile.

The house smelled of sizzling meat and garden seasonings, which would have stirred the rider's hunger if she were not so thirsty. "Do you have any water?" she asked, licking her chapped lips.

"Why yes, of course." The woman went into the kitchen for what felt like several minutes but was likely only a few seconds and came back with a gleaming glass of water with several spheres of ice floating at the top.

The rider chugged the glass down in one gulp, welcoming brain freeze for the first time in her life.

"We don't get many travelers out here in Stormgate, bein' that we're in the middle of nowhere. But when we do, y'all come in hungry, thirsty and bone-weary." All of the sudden, the woman's smile turned into a glare of skepticism and concern, a similar look the rider had received from the veterinarian and the passing riders on the street. "Um, what can I do for ya?"

"I need a room."

"Of course." She reached for the reddish-brown leather book on the entryway table next to one of the rocking chairs. "We have shared rooms for two platinum a night. And a private room for five platinum a night. Which would you—"

"I'll take the private room." She reached into her pocket to the sound of delicate clinking, handed the manager three platinum coins and pointed up the lightly finished wooden stairs. "The room is up here, I take it?"

"No baggage?" asked the manager.

"No."

"You handed me fifteen platinum. Are you plannin' on stayin' three nights with us?"

"Until my trugan is healed. If I'm gone in a night or two, you can keep the extra coin."

"I see. Oh, and I didn't catch your name, dear."

"Kasta Krane." The rider stopped in her tracks and rolled her eyes. 'You idiot,' she thought. 'You gave your real name. Why did you give your real name?' The young woman reached into her pocket again and put another ten platinum on top of the manager's open book. "For your trouble," she said. "And to keep quiet if anyone asks for me."

"Oh, young miss, that really isn't necessary."

"Please," said the rider. "I insist."

As the petite woman in red looked up at the tall woman in black, she swallowed, then cleared her throat. "Of course." She closed the book. "Welcome to the Stormgate Boarding House. We will have a meal prepped in the next hour. Will you be joinin' us?"

"Can you just send some meat and fruit up to my room?"

"If you would prefer, young miss. If you would prefer." She handed her guest a brass key on a thin chain. "Second door on your right."

The rider in black stepped up the stairs and stomped across the faded blue rug in the narrow hallway. She slid the key into the lock on the pearl-white wooden door. After entering the room, she slammed the door shut behind her, breathing heavily as her back thumped against the wall. The quarters were tight and contained sparse decoration. There was a single weaved rug on the floor with a cactus and geometric patterns. A tall lamp with a smoky flower-shaped shade sat atop a circular nightstand beside a twin bed. A single window overlooked the street, cracked open about a half inch.

She stomped into the water closet, barely big enough for her to turn around in. There was no shower. The showers were in a larger washroom down the hall, a space she would share with other guests of the boarding house. The rider looked in the mirror. Covering her blue-grey face was a streak of blood. It was not hers. It was not the cougar's. It was...

That scream, that anguished scream. Why did he have to—?

She shook out the terrible thoughts from her head and stuck her face under the sink. Her calloused hands harshly scrubbed until every streak of reddish brown was washed away. She looked to the mirror again, then looked away. She could not stand the sight of herself. Clutching the handle of her pistol, she stepped out of the water closet. Oh, how she wanted to shower, but she could not bring herself to leave the room. She locked the door. After removing her vest, her belt and her boots, she collapsed on top of the bed. The sound of galloping trugan faded in and out on the street below. Her eyes grew heavy as she released a long breath. The woman in black drifted off, keeping her pistol aimed on the door.

Kasta awoke with a shiver, despite the stuffy aridity of her desert quarters. It was dark out. She had slept through the entire day, other than the brief interlude she took to eat the meal that the boarding house manager had brought to her. She heard the other guests walking downstairs, no doubt gathering around the table for dinner. Kasta decided that this would be the perfect time to sneak into the communal washroom for shower access.

The showerheads were three feet away from one another, separated by circular beige curtains. The water was burning hot, then freezing cold. She had little control over the temperature; it seemed to alter with a will of its own. While the water never remained at a consistent, comfortable temperature, it did provide a sense of purification, like the dread of the night, and of her former life was washing away.

'What do I do now?' she thought. 'What is out there for someone like me in that terrible, hungry world?'

She looked at the drain, solemnly spinning as it swallowed the filth of her sins. She would have to change her name, the way she talked, even her appearance. Perhaps she could hop on a ship and move to Rogue Haven. They would never find her there.

Would they?

She shut off the water, dried off and covered herself with a towel. She put on her clothes, which were still dirty, behind the curtain. Tomorrow there would be time to wash them or buy new garments. Peeking each direction down the hallway before stepping out, she scurried back to her room.

There, she waited. She waited until the sounds of chatter and merriment ceased. When it was finally quiet, she crept down the creaking wooden stairs and stepped into the kitchen. The manager of the boarding house was sitting with one elbow on the table, swirling a whisky glass.

"Good evenin' to ya," she said with a casual wave, as though she were expecting Kasta. "Comin' down for a bite to eat?"

"Yeah," replied Kasta with a crack in her voice. "I know I'm late. I just—"

"No need to explain. Hope you're alright with desert hen and sour cactus salad." She took a sip of whisky.

"Yeah, that sounds good."

"Make yourself a plate, dear. It's all still on the counter."

Kasta did as instructed, taking mountainous portions of the greasy bird meat and blue-leafed salad drenched in aromatic green dressing. She eyed the unmarked bottle of whisky on the counter. "Mind if I have a glass of that?"

The woman turned around, the creases of her face following her frown. "That ain't included with your room and board."

"That's fine. How much?"

"Let's call it one platinum per glass."

Kasta reached into her pocket and flipped the elder woman a coin. She caught the shimmering unit of currency and flipped over a clean glass that rested near the bottle. Careful to pour Kasta no more than a single shot, she presented the beverage to the young woman, along with a skeptical glare. "I'd reckon you're too young to be drinkin', but I would hedge my bets this ain't your first dance with the bottle."

Kasta shook her head.

"Cheers," said the woman as their glasses clinked together.

Kasta sat down to eat. She found the flavors of the bird and the vegetables overwhelming. She thought this might be the best meal she had ever eaten in her life. But she could not be certain, as she felt the need to swallow each bite before fully tasting it.

"By the way," said the older woman. "Your name is Jessel."

"What?" mumbled Kasta, her mouth full.

"Your name is Jessel. Some of the other guests were asking about you. So, I gave them your name. The name that *you* gave me this mornin' when you checked in." Her head tilted as she spoke through an assured grin. "Your name *is* Jessel, yes?"

"No." Kasta shook her head and washed down her mouthful of meat with a swig of whisky. "Everyone calls me Jess."

"Pleased to meet ya, Jess," the manager said with a bow of her head. "I'm Ryna."

Kasta nodded and continued to indulge. "Pleased to meet ya."

In the middle of the night, Kasta lay in bed. She had managed to fall asleep after some tossing, turning and flipping of the pillow to find the cooler side. But she was thrust out of her slumber by the sound of an approaching trugan outside the boarding house. The galloping slowed, then halted. Through the window, she heard someone dismount. Heavy boots met the wooden patio with a hollow resonance.

Thump. Thump. Thump.

They stopped for a moment. Perhaps he was turning around. But then the steps became clearer, louder, closer.

Thump. Thump. Thump.

The night turned silent for what seemed like an eternity. Kasta's breath stopped as she pulled the scratchy blankets tight to her body.

Knock, knock, knock.

The rider was at the door. 'It's just a passer in the night, looking for lodging,' Kasta told herself. 'It's not them. It's not…'

Knock, knock, knock.

The wrapping became louder, faster and more aggressive.

Knock-knock-knock-knock-knock-knock.

The door opened. "Can I help you?" asked Ryna, weary irritation in her voice.

"Top of the evening to ya, ma'am."

Kasta gasped. She reached for her pistol on the nightstand. She knew that deep, trembling voice. It was Dead-Eye Daslund, one of the gang's top hunters. They were here. They had found her.

He continued. "I'm a bounty hunter. I'm looking for a fugitive and have reason to believe that she may have passed through these parts. Have you seen this woman? Her name is Kasta Krane. She's armed, dangerous and a threat to any who cross her path."

"Hmm." Ryna clicked her tongue. "She doesn't look familiar."

They had a digital image of her. They were showing people her like-ness. She had to get out. She had to get out now. She could burst through the window and fire on him, then steal his trugan. She could ride into the night for the western coast. But what if he was not alone? What if there were more waiting in the street, or outside of town?

Plus, she could not abandon Kai. She would never be able to live with herself.

'If I'm going down, it's going to be right here,' she thought. 'And I'll go down fighting.'

Daslund's dry cackle echoed through the window, stealing Kasta's breath. "Mind if I get a look at your logs?" he asked.

"I actually do mind," replied Ryna. "This is a private business and you are no law official. So, unless you can come back with a warrant from Marshal Tollimson, who happens to be a good friend of mine, you can stay right there."

"Oh, I can assure you that my business is quite legitimate," he said with a slithering civility in his voice. "I can come back with the proper documentation. But you'd really be savin' me a lot of trouble if—"

"Good, do that! Come back with a warrant from... I'm sorry, what department did you say you were hired by?"

"Um—Ox Well."

"*Oh*, of course!" Ryna's voice rose in pitch, a sudden influx of cheer in her tone. "How is Marshal Dharma, anyway?"

"He's well," replied Daslund. "His department is always a pleasure to work with."

"Marshal Dharma is a woman," replied Ryna, a purring growl beneath her words. "And she's not the marshal of Ox Well. She's the Marshal of Mosswood Port. Good day, sir."

The creaking door began to shut, but it was stopped with a loud thump.

"Move your foot," ordered Ryna.

"Listen," said Daslund, a hostile chill in his words. "I don't wish to bring harm to an old woman, but..."

"Don't worry, you won't be."

Those bootsteps slid backward. "Easy, ma'am, I really just want to talk. We don't need no trouble. Put the rifle down."

"Get on your trugan and get out of this town. We don't want your kind here, *bandit*."

"I'm a bounty hunter. I already told you."

"Sure ya are." His steps continued to retreat as she spoke. "Go do your bounty huntin' someplace else. If I ever see ya out around my boarding house again, I'll call in the marshal."

"Give me a room." His voice now came from the street. "I need a place to rest. Been riding through the night.

"No vacancy," replied Ryna as she slammed the door shut and latched all the locks.

Kasta gripped her pistol tight during the ensuing silence. She heard him returning to his saddle. He shouted, "Look me up if you see her!" He let out a guttural laugh. "If she lets you live long enough. Don't say I didn't warn ya."

Kasta held her breath as she left her pistol aimed at the window. Her finger tapped the trigger. Her hand shook. She did not take a breath until the gallop of his trugan faded into the soft breeze of the desert. Though she would not sleep any more that night, her unrest was somewhat settled knowing that Ryna was downstairs.

Blue rays of daylight pierced the windows of the stable. Kaiar hopped in place when she saw Kasta enter. With a smile of relief, Kasta ran to her steed and wrapped her arms around her neck.

The old vet approached, wiping his hands with a wet cloth. "This is the happiest I have seen her since you brought her in. That trugan really loves you, young lady."

"We've been through a lot together," said Kasta, brushing her finger down Kai's snout. The beast closed her eyes in contentment.

"I can see that." He leaned over and pointed to the beast. "I cleaned, dressed and sealed her wounds. That cougar y'all tussled with sure did a number." He took off his hat and fanned his face. "I have her on a few relaxants and pain suppressors. If she's a little loopy, that's why."

"Aww," said Kasta with a grin. "Are you drugged up, girl?"

The beast's tongue flicked as she rested her head on Kasta's shoulder.

"I just need to add another layer of temporary grafting to her stomach. And she should be ready to leave by tomorrow morning."

Kasta's body tensed. "How much will it run me to have her ready to go today?"

"No." The man held out his arms and shook his head. "It's not about money. She's not ready. She needs another night's rest to—"

"Forty platinum? Fifty platinum?" She reached into her pocket and began to separate coins.

"You really are in a hurry, ain't ya?"

"What gave you that idea?"

He sighed and crossed his arms. "Forty platinum is fine."

She took four coins and dropped them in his hand, giving Kaiar a final pat on the head before turning to leave.

"I don't suppose you'd happen to be in the bounty database, would you?"

Kasta froze in her steps and looked over her shoulder. "Come again?"

"If I go into the marshal's office and take a look at the bounty board, I won't find you on there, will I?"

She sneered and continued walking. "Old timer, if I *were* a criminal, you still wouldn't find me on a wanted poster."

"You're that good, huh?"

"You're damn right." She turned the corner, leaving the veterinarian's company. "Tell me when she's ready."

Kasta's boots waded through the dirt roads. A faint breeze brought with it a tumbleweed, bouncing in the opposite direction. After navigating the mostly empty avenue, she stepped through the swinging doors of the saloon. She sat at the wooden bar, sticky all the way across. The chair screeched as she leaned against the tarnished backrest. A pungent smell of body odor hung over the establishment, despite her, the bartender and two other patrons being the only ones present.

"What can I get for ya?" asked the bartender, forcing a smile on her frail purple lips. She wore a white sleeveless top. Her forearms were so blue they could have passed for the skin tone of an Islander, but her shoulders were so grey that they looked to belong to a Vandeni from the far north, or even an Imperial.

Kasta looked around for a menu, either on the bar, on one of the tables or on a board behind the counter, but did not find one. "Oh, um..." She shrugged. "What do you have to eat?"

"Eggs, bacon..."

Kasta leaned forward, expecting more options. But the list ended there. "Okay. How about eggs and bacon, then?"

"One hundred fifty electrum."

Kasta squinted in confusion. She had never heard anyone phrase a total owed that way before. Usually, one would simply say one platinum fifty. "How much is a cup of coffee?"

"Fifty electrum."

Again, most people would have just said half a platinum. 'I really am in the middle of nowhere.'

She dropped two shimmering coins on the counter. "Two platinum. Coffee with the bacon and eggs, please."

The bartender swept up the coins and scampered to the kitchen without another word. Kasta considered ordering a whisky, but she could simply buy another glass off Ryna for a single platinum. Plus, her coin pocket was getting lighter. And she still had to pay a cybernetics engineer to finish work on Kai when she got to the next town. Where was the next town anyway? What was she going to do there? What was she going to do once she *left* the next town?

Kasta sipped her coffee, overwhelmed by the questions she asked of herself. 'Why can't I just... live?' she thought. 'Is life supposed to be this terrifying?'

The swinging doors opened. Kasta snuck a glance over her shoulder, letting her hand drop to the handle of her pistol. A thick man's silhouette stood in the blue-cast shadow of Athenis. He took a slow step forward, then another.

Kasta let out a quiet sigh of relief when she saw that it was not Daslund, nor any of the others who pursued her. But when he bounced off the back of her chair and made her spill coffee on her lap, she clenched her teeth and shook her head.

He pulled out a chair two seats over from Kasta and stumbled into it, barely able to maintain balance on the footrest. "Agnissa!" he yelled. "Get out here. I want me a whisky."

Kasta groaned and let her hair fall into her face, hiding her eyes.

The bartender stomped out from the kitchen, puffing out a sigh. "Malerand, I ain't serving you a drop until you settle your tab. You're seventy-five platinum deep, ya hear? Plus, it looks to me like you've already had plenty."

He stumbled into the seat he had pulled out, barely able to brace himself against the bar. "You ain't my momma. You're the bartender." He tugged on his greasy, unevenly trimmed mustache. "Do yer damn job and pour me a drink."

"Get out," said Agnissa. "And get help."

"You can't tell me what to do. My great grandpappy built this town!"

"And *you've* contributed nothin' to it."

He locked his hands together, leaning across the bar. "Please, Aggie, just one whisky. I swear I'll pay ya back. I got a lot tied up in investments right now. Once they's paid off, I'll pay ya back everything plus interest. I swear it."

Agnissa shook her head. "I'm calling the marshal." She stepped back to the kitchen.

Kasta could feel the sweaty, burly man's eyes on her. She turned away, sipping on her coffee.

"Hey, you," he said, a growl beneath his words.

'Just ignore him,' thought Kasta. 'Ignore him and he'll lose interest.'

"I said hey... you." Lumbering steps squeaked against the wooden floor.

'Just pretend he is not there. I don't want to draw any more attention to myself right now, not with Daslund patrolling the region.'

His hand slapped against the back of her chair. "I'm talking to you, young lady..."

Kasta's fingers clutched the handle of her pistol.

"Don't you know that you're supposed to mind your elders?"

With her other hand, she took a sip of coffee. "Is that right?"

"You playing smart with me?"

"You playing dumb with me?" She turned to face him, her hair covering one eye. "Or is this just... how you are?"

"You better start showing me some respect."

She turned away. "I don't have time for this right now. Piss off."

He leaned low, bracing a hand against the back of her chair. "What'd you say to me?" His breath smelt of cinnamon whisky and oysters.

"Hey, Malerand," one of the patrons at the table yelled. "Leave the young lady alone. She didn't do nothin' to ya."

The other chimed in. "Get out of here before Marshal Tollimson arrests ya. Again."

He looked to them with a belch before turning back to Kasta. "Seems I'm not welcome here," he whispered.

Kasta raised an eyebrow. "You're quite observant."

"So just buy me a whisky and I'll be on my way."

Kasta shook her head. "That's not happening."

"I said..."

Kasta saw him reaching for his belt, no doubt for a weapon. Her instinct was to draw her shock-cannon and fire on the man before he had a chance. But she wished to avoid cannon fire if possible, for the sound carried for miles. If Daslund, or any of the gang heard it, they would come to investigate. And she would have to leave town without Kaiar.

"Buy. Me. A whisky." He held an old rusty pistol at his side.

"No."

He pointed the cannon at her. Every cybernetic in her nervous system began firing off. Every reflex, informed by her bodily augments, warned of the danger. If his finger touched that trigger, she would have no choice but to fire upon him.

'No,' she thought. 'No cannon fire.'

She sighed and reached for the porcelain cup of coffee. "Get that weapon out of my face."

"Or what?"

"Or I'll give you that drink you want so badly."

His eyes squinted in confusion before he erupted in spitting laughter. She felt the mist of saliva on the back of her neck and saw it rain into her cup of coffee. Shaking with anger, she spun around in her chair. With her right hand, she smashed the cup into his face, shattering the porcelain and immediately burning the wounds with hot coffee. Then, with her left hand, she grabbed ahold of the drunken man's arm and twisted it backward. She did not mean to break the bone, just to disarm him. But when she turned his elbow toward his back, she heard a loud snap. The other patrons winced and let out a collective "oooh."

As Malerand fell to his knees, screaming in agony, Kasta locked a boot to his back and forced him to the ground. He whimpered and attempted to break free, but she pulled his arm farther back. "Don't move!" she ordered, kicking him to the floor.

At that moment, the marshal walked in. He was an older man with a silver mustache and a reddish-brown hat. "What in the name of the Guardians is going on in here?" he asked, drawing his weapon.

"Marshal!" shouted Malerand, attempting to slither from Kasta's grip. "This no-good desert drifter attacked me! Everyone saw it. I want to press charges!"

'Damn it,' Kasta thought. 'They're going to arrest me for taking down this local boy. I'm gunna have to shoot the marshal and get out of here.' She reached for her pistol. 'I'll just incap him. I can't go to jail...'

"Malerand was causing trouble again," said one of the patrons. "The drifter woman put him in his place."

The other patron laughed.

The marshal stepped forward, hands in his belt as he studied Kasta. She swallowed. "I'll be damned, young lady." He studied the hold that she had the large man in, one arm behind his back and her boot pinning him to the floor. "Looks like you had an easier time taking down the big fella than I do when he starts actin' up. What department you with?"

"Umm—what?"

"What badge you wear?" He flashed her a thin smirk. "Are you one of Leason's? Aberthine's? Dharma's?" He cleared his throat, looking over his shoulder before he whispered, "You're not one of Jos', are you?" He eyed her leather garb and asymmetrical haircut. "You do kinda have that Vulture air about ya."

"Ummm... I... I..."

"That's alright." He waved her off with a chuckle. "You ain't gotta tell me. I don't like to talk about work when I'm off duty neither." He stepped beside Kasta and grabbed ahold of Malerand's other arm. "I can take him from here. But I do appreciate ya helping to deescalate this situation, even though ya are off duty." He locked the disorderly suspect in electro-chains before standing him up. "Though if I were on vacation, this ain't where I'd come."

Kasta shrugged. "I'm just passing through."

"That's pretty much why this town is here," the marshal said. "Just to pass through." He walked the suspect toward the door. "Ya gotta be a special kind of person to find yourself stayin' put in these parts, don't ya, Malerand?"

"Just take me to Doctor Bora."

"We're going to book ya at the department first, Mal. Disorderly conduct, attempted assault, probably a few others. We'll see."

"What?!" He whimpered as the marshal shoveled him along. "But that little minx broke my arm."

"And it'll still be broken after we book ya." As the marshal swung the doors open, he turned and tipped his hat to Kasta. "Thanks again."

Kasta nodded and let out a deep breath, clutching the sides of the bar.

Agnissa stepped back out from the kitchen, her wide green eyes locked on Kasta.

"How much do I owe you for the cup?" asked Kasta, reaching into her coin pocket.

"Are you kiddin'?" Agnissa leaned over the bar with a wide grin. "Breakfast is on the house, sug."

The veterinarian informed Kasta that Kaiar would be ready to leave in an hour, after the grafting on her wounds fully dried. He made her promise not to ride her faster than seventy-five miles per hour until her cybernetics were repaired. Kasta agreed.

On a rocking chair on the terrace outside the boarding house, Ryna smoked a cigarillo.

"Mind if I buy one of those off you?" asked Kasta.

Ryna reached into her blouse and handed Kasta one of the thin rolls of tobacco. "Cigarillos are included with lodging, dear."

"Really?"

"For you, yes."

Kasta smiled as she used her utility tool to light the cigarillo. "I heard you, by the way."

"Heard what, dear?"

"Last night…" She bowed her head and gestured to the entrance of the boarding house. "I heard you covering for me when that man knocked on the door."

Ryna shooed away the notion and pursed her lips. "That was nothin'."

"Not to me." Kasta struggled to say what she wanted to. "Why'd you help me?"

"Oh, child." She mixed her tea and took a drag from her cigarillo. "When you've been around as long as I have, you learn to recognize a good person runnin' from a bad place. And you learn to recognize a man who don't mean no good."

"He's very dangerous," uttered Kasta. "I'm just… I'm glad he didn't try to force his way past you."

Ryna gave a raspy chuckle. "One look at my pappy's rifle and he went runnin' off. Can't be that dangerous."

Kasta laughed along but looked away to hide her darkened shift in mood. For Ryna's sake, Kasta had to make sure she was not there if Daslund did return. Next time, he would not knock.

"Thanks for everything," she said as she stepped down the stairs. "I best be off."

"Where ya headin'?"

Kasta paused. She did not want to give away too much information about her future destination, even though she trusted Ryna enough. "Not sure yet. Somewhere that I can get my trugan fixed up."

"If you are going to Ox Well, you won't make it all the way in a day's ride on a lame trugan. Be sure to stop in Shadowfall Canyon on the way. I know the man who runs the boarding house up there. Tell him I sent ya. He'll give ya a fine rate."

Kasta smiled and nodded. "I will."

"And be sure to stop by again. Consider the extra coin you left me with a down payment. If you ever feel like settlin' in these parts, I know that Marshal Tollimson would shine a deputy badge for ya personally."

Kasta nodded.

"So long, Jess."

"It's Kasta."

Ryna's eyes widened. "Oh, is it now?"

"It is."

"Glad to hear it, dear. Glad to hear it."

After returning to the vet's stable, Kasta sat atop Kaiar's saddle. She gave the beast a pat on the head and a scratch on the chin. "What do you think, Kai? Think we can handle another ride?"

Kaiar grunted in a passionate affirmative.

Kasta said farewell to the vet. When she and Kai reached the main street of Stormgate, they took off at a high speed, but not maximal speed.

"We can stop if you need a rest, girl," Kasta whispered in her mount's ear. "Don't push yourself too hard."

Kaiar hissed with enthusiasm.

The rider in black rode across the desert plains under the infinite wonder of the violet sky. A smile rested on her face as the ranges of indigo cacti welcomed her with open arms. She looked over her shoulder. No one followed. And even if they did follow, they would not catch her. She looked at the cloudless purple sky and the brilliant blue of Athenis as it reached for the amber sands. The Vanden desert would lead her where it pleased, an endless offer of possibility for anything and anyone who accepted.

THE CASE OF THE GILL RIPPER
I. Sleep is for the Dead

'Not in my town.'

Deputy Raelyn Bovien's boots thumped against the old, hollow stairs. She held on to her hat as sweat dripped from her hairline to her forehead. Harsh winds shrilled through the streets of Barren Rock, burned by the blue rays of daylight. Dust propelled from the cracks of the floorboards and dissipated into the shrieking gusts.

'No one spills blood in my town without answer.' She reached the top of the stairs and set foot on the flat deck. 'You will not spill another drop.' With a step forward, the automatic metal door opened. Raelyn took a deep breath and stepped inside the building. 'Not a drop.'

"Deputy Bovien!" the bouncy voice of Grig shouted from behind his wooden desk. "Where have you been? The marshal was expecting you twenty minutes ago!"

Raelyn sighed. She removed her hat as the automatic door sealed behind her. "I know." With a smack of her brown hat, a cloud of dust scattered from the brim. "I lost track of time."

Grig stumbled, thrusting a full glass of water toward Raelyn. "Here."

The deputy's bloodshot eyes strained as she grabbed the overflowing glass. Though still sore, it did give her dry throat some relief. She grunted and wiped her lips with the sleeve of her jacket.

"Well, get in there," the man said, taking the glass back.

"Okay." She pulled back her red hair and dropped her hat atop her head. "How do I look?" she asked.

"Like you haven't bathed in a day nor slept in two."

Deputy Bovien stamped toward the hallway. "I'd be angry if you weren't right, Grig."

Grig chuckled, stepping back to his desk.

Raelyn's lips twisted. Her palms turned sweaty. She sighed, approaching the end of the hallway, then cracked her knuckles with her thumb before twisting the doorknob. "I'm so sorry I'm late—"

Marshal Zeller pressed his index finger to his purple lips, halting her words. Deputy Bovien winced, inching the door shut. Her face tightened as the latch clicked back in place with the grace of crashing thunder. Her superior was too distracted to notice or care.

"But I don't think any of the suspects you got in custody match up with the evidence we have, Marshal Zeller," a muffled voice said through the speaker on the desk. "They ain't got the surgical and anatomical knowledge to commit this type of murder."

Zeller let out a short sigh. "Jos, just because you guys in Vulture got it in your head that the killer is a doctor, it doesn't mean it's true. We're going to consider all possibilities."

"Well, maybe not a doctor," Jos replied. "But definitely not an old merchant or an unschooled drifter."

Deputy Bovien wrapped her hand around the chair opposite Marshal Zeller's. "I agree that the murderer likely has a comprehensive knowledge of anatomy. Such a thorough dissection requires years of practice," she said. She pulled the chair out and sat down, her hands crossed over the top of the desk. "At least, according to our medical examiners."

Marshal Jos' voice crackled through the speaker. "Deputy Bovien! I was glad to hear you were on the case. We have been closing in on this butcher for months. He must have *known* we were close, because now he's fled to the other side of the continent."

"How do we know this isn't just a copycat? Like the murder a few days ago in Duneland?" Zeller said, locking his fingers behind his head. His white eyebrows lowered. "The ongoing investigation of 'The Vulture Gill Ripper' has become quite the phenomenon around all of Vanda, ya know?"

"Could be," Jos said, clearing his throat. "But I don't think it's likely."

"Neither do I," Raelyn said, eying the speaker that projected Jos' voice. "The stab and slice wounds, the manner in which the vital organs were extracted, even the position of the body." She swallowed as Marshal Zeller sneered at her. "It's all identical to your department's case file, Jos."

"I thought it may be," Jos said. "Well, my office will help in any way we can. Which is why I've sent my lead investigator from the Vulture case to give you some assistance."

Deputy Bovien shook her head. "Jos, please tell me it's not that hot-shot deputy that has been stirring up trouble everywhere she steps."

"I know she may not be the most orthodox law official," Jos was swift to reply. "But what she lacks in grace, she makes up for in efficiency. I guarantee it."

Marshal Zeller nodded. "A joint investigation between Barren Rock and Vulture will help us get to the bottom of this. We'll put this monster behind bars before he hurts someone else."

Background noise and static flowed through the speaker. "I gotta run. But my deputy should be there within the next few hours. Sorry this curse has to come to your town, but I wish you two the best of luck."

The transmission disconnected. Zeller leaned forward. His hazy brown eyes hid behind a long blink. But his gaze still penetrated Raelyn. "Why were you late, Deputy?"

Raelyn cleared her throat. Her spine tensed and her fingertips tightened around the armrest. "I was at the scene."

"All night?"

"Yeah."

Marshal Zeller slumped back. "Well, get some rest. We have the three suspects in custody. Deputy Colverg is taking a crack at interrogation."

Raelyn sighed. "Colverg? He's not gunna do anything. Send me in."

"Later," Zeller said. His eyes turned to the electronic data system on his desk. "For now, you rest."

Deputy Bovien thought up a rebuttal—but bit her tongue. "Yessir," she said with a nod.

The deputy left the room and went to her office. She closed the door, sat down, and opened the case file on her data system entitled "City of Vulture: Gill Ripper Murders."

She scrolled through the file, reviewing the crime scenes. The screen flooded with images of young women. A pit formed in Raelyn's stomach as she thought of their final moments, how filled with dread they must have been. She pondered their families; not a day would pass without a strike of grief for the rest of their lives. With a whimper, she turned her head away and shut her eyes.

But the deputy swallowed her sorrow and looked to the screen, and the pictures of the victims stared back. 'I will catch him,' she thought. 'I'll rest when you can rest.'

"Deputy," a sharp voice said, followed by three knocks.

Raelyn jumped in her seat and looked across her office. Grig peeked from behind the creaking door. She forced her heavy eyelids open and adjusted her hat. "Yeah?" she said, clearing her throat.

"There is a woman outside. Says she is from the Vulture Law Department."

"Okay." She fidgeted. Her brown leather chair screeched as she leaned into the backrest. "I'll be right out."

'How long was I asleep?' The deputy's thoughts raced as she forced herself to her feet. 'How did she make it so fast? How much of the case file did I read? Did I read any? I can't remember.' She stepped out of her office and trudged down the hall.

The late afternoon rays of blue starlight attacked her eyes as she stepped outside. Her thin brown shirt stuck to her sweaty amphibious skin. She gave her collar a light tug, sending a breeze down her chest.

A woman in black led her reptilian beast through the street, leaving it in front of the trough. The tip of a silver badge peeked out from the pocket of her black leather jacket. After patting her mount's head, she turned toward the stairs. Her cyan eyes narrowed on Deputy Bovien.

Raelyn remembered her name from the Vulture case file. "Deputy Krane," she said with a wide, forced smile. "Welcome to the city of Barren Rock. I am Deputy Raelyn Bovien, and I'm pleased to have your assistance on this case."

Deputy Krane stomped up the stairs, paying no attention to Raelyn's extended hand. "Hey," Krane said as she passed.

A tingle passed down Raelyn's spine, which she shook out through her fingertips. She let out a sigh. Grig evaded Deputy Krane's gait as he stepped outside.

"Grig," Raelyn said, followed by a second sigh. "Please get me a cup of coffee."

Grig nodded and turned around with a soft smile.

Raelyn stepped into the lobby. Deputy Krane stared down the hallway. "So, I hear you got three suspects," she said, twisting toward Raelyn. "I'm gunna need to talk to them."

Deputy Bovien closed her beige eyes, resting her hands on her hips. "Well, hold on, we have to discuss—"

"Nothing to discuss. Lemme get in there and I'll get a confession. If any of them did it."

Raelyn stepped forward. "Deputy Krane, I have an ongoing investigation here. I welcome you to be a part of it, but you're not just going to take it over."

Deputy Krane took a step toward Raelyn in turn. "That's the problem. It's ongoing. I'm here to change that."

Bovien's heel rapped against the wooden floor. "Well, you couldn't change that in Vulture, could you?"

Deputy Krane crossed her arms. Her purple lips compressed into a tight line. "Months of investigation have led me here. I'm not about to let some tin badges in a one-trugan town screw this up."

"Okay," Bovien said with a slight smile. Her eyes locked with Krane's. "Don't you want to at least see the crime scene first?" She relaxed her stance and extended her forearm. "How did you even get here so fast, Krane? It's a long way from Vulture, even by airship."

"I didn't fly," Krane said, eyes slanting toward the ceiling. Her finger tapped the handle of her pistol. "And I didn't come from Vulture. I was in Duneland, investigating the other murder." She turned her gaze back to Raelyn. "And call me Kasta."

"Okay. Kasta." Raelyn again went to shake the Vulture deputy's hand. Her arm protruded for several moments, her thin lips refusing to let go of the slight smile that she forced on them. Kasta did nothing but clasp her own arm, glowering at Raelyn's hand as if it were roadkill. "And you can call me Raelyn if you wish."

Kasta let go of her own arm and grabbed a tight hold of Raelyn's hand. Too tight. "Doesn't matter what you want me to call you. I'm probably not gunna remember."

'By the blue rays of Athenis, she's worse than I imagined,' Raelyn thought.

Grig approached from behind and handed Raelyn her coffee. Before she could thank him, Kasta snapped her gloved finger. "Get me one of those too, will ya? Black."

Grig's eyes rolled from side to side. "Certainly," he said with a dramatic turn.

"Well, *Deputy*," Kasta said with a sneer. "You gunna show me this crime scene of yours?"

Raelyn Bovien took a sip of her coffee, standing tall with her chest forward. "Whenever you're ready. *Deputy*."

II. A Killer's Mark

"So, are you nervous?" Kasta lit a cigarillo, circling the dry puddle of blood.

"About what?" Raelyn asked, standing in the middle of the alleyway. "That the killer got away?" A hot breeze touched the back of her neck.

"No, that you have a killer at all." The young deputy's laugh was coarser than the crunch of gravel beneath her boots. "It's your first month as a deputy-detective, and you already got a murder on your hands."

Raelyn looked to her mobile data system. "If the people of Vulture could deal with you letting a deranged individual kill so many people—" She bit her tongue and let out a sharp sigh. Her tone had turned hostile. She would not sink to this deputy's—this *child's* level. "I trust the township of Barren Rock will be just as accommodating as we proceed with our investigation."

"They won't," Kasta said through a cloud of smoke. "Vulture is a crazy town full of crazy people. Something tells me that the people of this little desert den don't see stuff like this too often." Her purple lips twisted. "They probably think it's your fault."

'Ignore her. Just focus on the case. She doesn't know what she's talking about. By the starlight of Athenis, does she know anything?' Raelyn Bovien cycled through images of the murder scene on her data system. She did not need to look at them. The victim's blood-soaked body had burned its way into the deepest part of her mind. Her disfigured face drowned her thoughts, frozen in an endless scream.

Raelyn's blue-grey Vandeni skin shuddered with a surge of goosebumps. "I'm sending you the crime scene pictures," she said with a shake of her head. "Along with the autopsy reports."

Kasta lowered her optical system from the top of her hat. She looked at the scene of the crime on the small screen before her eyes. "Okay," she said, leaning toward the dry pool of blood. "Victim is twenty-seven years old. Sex: Female. Species: Posaedian Vandeni. Barren Rock resident. Worked at the Corner Cactus Saloon." Her bright eyes crept toward Bovien. "Bartender? Escort?"

"Waitress." Bovien crossed her hands behind her back.

"Waitress..." Kasta looked down again. "There were no reports of screaming or disturbance. No reports of any suspicious activity in the saloon."

"Correct."

"Her body was discovered approximately one hour after the estimated time of death, by a passerby?"

"Yes. Bovorra of Kathmog, the local gemsmith. Her shop is on the main street."

"Okay," Kasta said. She paused, looking through her optical system. "Her gills were completely removed? Cut clean from her neck?"

"Yes. Her entire aquatic respiratory system was dissected and taken."

"And her eyes? Also removed?"

Raelyn Bovien sank to the young woman's level. "Nothing but empty sockets."

The digital display made a soft tone as Kasta studied the screen. "What else was removed?"

"Her tongue was cut clean from the throat. And her lips. They were—"

"Horrifying, right?" Kasta asked, taking a long drag from her cigarillo. "Turns your stomach."

"Yeah," Raelyn said with a shake of her head.

"Well, Deputy." Kasta's blue-grey face hid behind a cloud of smoke. "This ain't a copycat." She paused, staring at the puddle of blood once more. "It's him."

'Okay,' Raelyn thought. 'Maybe she does know what she's talking about.' "I've reviewed your department's files," she said, standing up straight. "I think you're right. The victim's profile, the crime scene, the manner in which dissection was conducted. The choice of organs taken..."

Kasta stood and walked toward Raelyn. "Yeah. I was just in Duneland. That was not him. *That* was a copycat. Some sicko trying to copy a sicko. And he didn't do a very good job. It was sloppy. Even their dumb law officials will figure that one out."

She paused, turning back toward the scene. "But this—this is him. And the Gill Ripper—he is not dumb. He leaves a body and disappears. Until another body pops up butchered the same way. It's like he only exists when he kills." Kasta spoke through clenched teeth. "After months of investigation in Vulture, we have no forensic evidence, no witnesses and no physical description of a suspect."

Raelyn's gaze narrowed on Kasta. "You guys think he's a doctor, right? Maybe selling the organs to black marketeers and cyberization engineers?"

Kasta shook her head. "I never bought into that."

Raelyn pointed at the Vulture deputy. "Because he leaves some of the most vital and valuable organs."

Kasta paused, her head tilting sideways. "Y-yes. Exactly." She walked away from the scene. "Brief me on everything else you've found here," she said, pulling on her lapels. "I want a crack at interrogating those three suspects you've got locked up."

Raelyn bit her lip and followed toward the end of the alleyway. "I'm sure you do."

III. In Witness of Unusual Suspects

The two women stood before three metal doors inside the marshal's department. "These are the three you picked up?" Kasta asked with a rapid shrug. "A scrap merchant, a local farmer and an amateur drifter?"

Raelyn crossed her arms. "They were the only ones passing through who ain't regular visitors."

The middle door opened. Deputy Colverg strolled from the room, closing the door behind him. Arrogance overflowed from his smirk. "It's Tivana Charrin. She did it."

"The drifter?" Raelyn asked.

"Oh yeah," Colverg said with a slow nod.

Kasta stepped his way, her black boots thumping against the creaking wooden floor. "So, you have a confession?"

"No," Colverg said, looking the young woman in black up and down. "I don't need one. She's acting all out of sorts. And she's the only one of the three who fits the profile." His snub nose crinkled as he forced his back straight. "Who are you, anyway?"

Kasta faced Raelyn, a crooked finger pointing toward Colverg. "He's an idiot, isn't he?"

Colverg's blue-grey face turned red, then white. His posture sank.

"Deputy Krane!" Raelyn gave Kasta a cold stare. "You will not speak that way about members of this department." Stepping toward her coworker, she spoke with a nervous shake beneath her words. "Forgive her, Colverg. She's a Vulture law official, sent to aid with the case." She forced a slight smile, which prompted Colverg to drop his guard. "Did you get any evidence that helps build a case against Charrin?" she asked.

"No."

"Okay," Raelyn Bovien said with a sigh. "Why don't you take a break? I'll give it a shot."

Colverg snarled and stomped down the hallway, not saying a word.

"Any reason you're defending the idiot?" Kasta asked, leaning against the wall.

Raelyn put her hands on her hips. Her eyes slanted toward Kasta. "Because he works in the same building as I do, Deputy Krane. I can't have you making me look bad in front of the people I work with."

Kasta leaned forward, speaking through a crooked grin. "My job isn't to worry about your workplace drama. It's to figure out who is brutally murdering people on both sides of Vanda."

"Well, maybe if you—" Three law officials passed by. Raelyn stopped and nodded, unsure whether she was smiling or frowning at them. She continued with a sharp whisper, "Maybe if you would consider your etiquette and work with me for a minute, we could catch this guy."

Kasta stepped in front of Raelyn, standing tall and looking down at her. "Maybe we could catch this guy if you stopped politicking with the idiots in your department and you let me interrogate these losers?"

Raelyn shook her head. "Fine. Let's get in there."

"Drifter first," Kasta said. She stepped toward the middle door. "I wanna see just how terrible of a case your small-town boy has built."

"Me too." Raelyn stepped forward and put her hand over the doorknob.

Kasta leaned in, her gloved finger extended. "So, he *is* an idiot."

Deputy Bovien's brow rose.

"I knew it."

Raelyn held back a chuckle and opened the door.

Inside the cubical chamber, a middle-aged woman sat at a metal desk. She tapped the surface, her yellow teeth breaking through her smile. Her cloak was tattered with the holes and shades of many dust storms. Her face was brown with dirt and oil. "Oh, by the grief of the Guardians." Her breath wafted across the room, heavy with a putrid mix of rum, eggs and onions. "They can't possibly be sending more of you. Can I just go? I don't know anything."

Kasta's feet shuffled against the floor. She stepped to the suspect's side, leaning low.

"She okay?" the drifter asked, her lip twitching.

Deputy Krane punched the table. "Why'd you do it?!" she screamed at the top of her lungs. "Why'd you kill the girl? Why'd you kill all those people back east? Tell me why or I'll shoot you dead right here!"

"Krane, stop!" Bovien screamed. But Kasta paid her no mind.

"I didn't do it," the suspect said, leaning as far back as the electro-chains binding her to the table would allow.

"We already know you did!" Deputy Krane slammed her fist against the table again. "Your prints are at the scene."

The suspect looked to Raelyn, words stuck in her throat behind quivering lips.

Kasta grabbed the woman's collar and pulled her up. "You better confess now. Or I'll put a cannon bolt in you right this minute."

"No, please I didn't do it! You gotta believe me."

Kasta's hand formed into a fist. She pulled her arm back. The suspect winced at the sight of the oncoming punch.

Raelyn leapt over the table and wrapped her arms around Kasta's back, the way she would a drunken aggressor in the saloon. She maintained her grip as Kasta struggled. The young girl was taller than Raelyn, but not strong enough to break her hold. Raelyn Bovien had held men twice her size in this grip.

"Let me go!" Kasta demanded, kicking her feet out. "I'm working here, damn it!"

"Calm down." Raelyn's embrace remained firm as she backed toward the exit. The drifter looked on in confusion and terror.

Raelyn reached out and opened the door. With one arm, she spun Kasta round and tossed her into the hall. The Vulture law official stumbled. But she regained her footing and made a break for the room.

Deputy Bovien slammed the door shut with a hard kick. Kasta banged on the metal door. "You haven't seen the last of me!" she shouted.

'Damn, this is embarrassing,' Bovien thought, looking back and forth down the hallway. Luckily, no one was present. "Hey!" she said, placing a hand on Kasta's shoulder. "Get ahold of yourself."

Kasta Krane pounded the door again. Bovien grabbed the woman's leather jacket and pinned her against the wall, propelled by a sudden swirl of rage. "Calm... the hell... down."

That stupid half grin climbed up her cheek again. "I am calm," Kasta said with an abrupt tone of cheerfulness. "Have you seen yourself?"

Deputy Bovien took a deep breath, and her anger passed. "Krane, you can't treat a Barren Rock suspect like that."

"I just did."

"You're weakening any potential case we could have!"

"She didn't do it anyway."

Raelyn scoffed. "So why be that aggressive?"

The young deputy pointed at Raelyn with her fingers in the shape of a pistol. "Fastest way to *confirm* she didn't do it. Scare the hell out of them. If they still maintain their innocence, they probably didn't do it."

Deputy Bovien looked down, shaking her head. "Or the fastest way to coerce someone into a false confession—under duress."

"Maybe," Kasta said with a shrug and purse of her lips. "But that's the court's problem. Not mine."

'I'm not gunna argue with this hotshot,' Raelyn thought. 'What a waste of time. There's a killer somewhere in my city. And I'm trying to pull this child off a poor defenseless nomad.'

"Wait here," she said with a grunt. "I'm going to try to rectify the damage that you just did."

"What do you mean?" Kasta crossed her arms. "I got what we wanted. She clearly didn't do it."

"Krane, that's not what I'm after." Raelyn put her hand on the door. "I want to know everything that she knows. Ask questions, find out where she was last night. See if she saw anything strange. Maybe she knows something that she doesn't wanna tell us." Deputy Bovien inclined her head toward Deputy Krane, her eyes wide and brow raised. "You know, detective work?"

Kasta Krane was silenced at last. Or did Raelyn slam the door so fast that the smart-ass did not have a moment to respond? She *also* slammed the door too hard; the suspect jolted at the sound.

'Deep breath.' Raelyn calmed herself with her thoughts. 'This poor woman does not need anyone else lashing out at her.'

The suspect's hands clutched the table. "Listen. I didn't kill the girl. I didn't do it. I swear!"

"Take it easy," Raelyn said with a smile, extending her hand. "And please forgive my colleague. She's from out of town. That was way out of line."

The suspect's dark blue eyes flickered. A tear fell down her cheek, which she wiped away with her shoulder. She stuttered, choking on her words.

'She's not sober,' Raelyn noted. 'I can use that to my advantage.' She motioned to the empty chair opposite the suspect. "Mind if I sit?"

The suspect shook her head.

Deputy Bovien kicked out the chair and sat down. "Can I offer you a cigarillo?"

Her eyes met Raelyn's for a moment—and she nodded. Raelyn always saved a cigarillo in her breast pocket. It helped keep her awake if she needed to pull an all-nighter. But in this case, it could help this woman feel a bit more comfortable.

Raelyn placed the cigarillo in the woman's mouth and lit the thin brown tip with her utility tool. "Now, Tivana Charrin. You say you didn't have anything to do with the waitress' death?"

"No. Nothing."

"Okay. I believe you. So, let's start at the beginning. What are you doing in Barren Rock? Where did you come from?"

Tivana reached up and pulled the cigarillo from her mouth. "What does that matter?"

Raelyn leaned forward. "Well, it matters a lot. You show up to our town a few nights before someone gets killed. People get suspicious. But I don't care about what people think. I wanna *know* what you know." The deputy's beige eyes shined with her smile. "Think you can help me with that, Miss Charrin?"

"You can call me Tiv." The drifter pulled her crimped, dangling hair away from her eyes, struggling against the tension of her binds. "Everyone calls me Tiv."

"Alright, Tiv." Marshal Bovien leaned forward. Her face broke through the veil of smoke. "And you can call me Raelyn."

"My last stop was Ash Valley. Before that, Eel's Mouth. I came here looking for work. And a fresh start. But I ain't had no luck with that."

"You been asking around?"

With a nervous nod, the drifter uttered, "Yeah."

Raelyn's head tilted sideways. "Where you been asking?"

Tiv looked down. "I dunno. The saloon."

"Well, maybe you shouldn't be spending all your time at the saloon there, Tiv." Raelyn offered a comforting smile.

"It's the only place I can..." The drifter stuttered and swallowed hard. "Never mind."

"Only place you can what, Tiv?"

Her eyes glazed over, and her pupils dilated, aimed at the corner of the room.

"It's okay, Tiv. You can tell me."

Tiv shook her head. "I'm not sayin' nothin'. You're a lawman. You'll bust me."

"Hey," Raelyn said, leaning toward her. "Barren Rock does not punish substance use or possession. Only the sale of a select few outside of declared establishments."

Her face somehow shined beneath the mask of oil. "Really?"

"Really."

This was only partially true. Barren Rock had banned the use of certain substances. Though most of the deputies did not enforce these laws with strict scrutiny, Marshal Zeller and some of the judges did like to make examples out of addicts, slapping them with harsh community service sentences. 'I'll just... leave this part out of my report,' Raelyn thought.

"Alright," Tiv said. "The smaller saloon on the main road... I can't remember the name."

"Corner Cactus."

"Yeah." Tiv gave a nervous nod. "That's where I've been getting it. The nebula."

"As in the proto-nebulous stimulant?" Raelyn asked.

The suspect nodded again.

"That *is* highly addictive, I've heard." Deputy Bovien gave the woman a sympathetic but reassuring grin. "I am sorry you're going through that. I see why you have been in the saloon. That's one substance that we aren't allowing to be sold right now. Not until we understand more about it."

Tiv sniffled, her breath trembling. "I came here *because* it ain't legal," she said. "I thought if I couldn't buy it from the local general store, I'd be able to get off it. But ain't no one gunna mind the law if there's a profit involved. It was just as easy to find a dealer in your saloon as it was to get a dose from a pharmacist in Ash Valley. And at least *their* supply ain't tainted..."

"Who in the saloon was selling you the stimulants, Tiv?" Raelyn's tone was stern.

Tiv's lip curled. "I ain't no rat!"

"I'm not busting anyone for the substance use, Tiv." Raelyn reached forward, palms out. "I'm just trying to get a clear picture of what may have been the scene of a horrible murder. Or at least the beginnings of one."

Tiv looked down, her cigarillo wet with saliva. "The waitress, what was her name?"

"Ella Lane."

"She was a nice girl. From what I saw of her."

"Did she give you the stims?"

"No!" Tiv stomped her feet on the floor. "Stop trying to trick me."

Raelyn's voice lowered in pitch but rose in volume. "Stop withholding information from this investigation. Or I'll send my colleague back in here."

Tiv tensed up. 'That was mean,' Raelyn thought. 'I shouldn't have said that.'

"It was one of the nighttime bartenders. Black hair, goatee, indigo eyes. I'm pretty sure he runs the whole operation."

Raelyn's eyes widened. 'That worked?' she thought. "I know exactly who that is. And don't worry, if he is ever punished for illegal sale of mind-altering substances, I will never report you as a witness."

"Thank you," Tiv said with a sigh.

Raelyn paused and leaned back. "So, were you at the saloon last night?"

"For a while, yeah."

"Tell me everything you remember."

"Well, it was the same as it had been the last several nights. Not too slow, but not all that busy either." The crow's feet branching from Tiv's eye twitched. "Some chatty fellows at the table next to me, which was messin' with my mood a bit."

"What about the victim? Did you see Ella at all?"

"Yeah, a couple times."

Raelyn sighed. "And how did she seem compared to other nights."

Tiv cleared her throat. "Like I said, I barely saw her. She looked maybe a little more annoyed—ummm—or stressed than usual." She looked down, bracing her arms. "Or maybe I am just remembering it that way because someone did her in. Waitresses in a place like that are always a bit bothered. Between the rude drunks, whistling cannonslingers and loitering bums like me, who could blame them?" Tiv bit her lip and forced a loud swallow. "I just wish it coulda been an ol' bum like myself to bite the dust. Not a young, pleasant girl like her." A sniffle escaped between her words. "Did she have any family?" she muttered.

"Yeah," Raelyn said with a nod. "A mom and a couple of brothers. Somewhere down south."

Tiv did not reply. She closed her eyes and folded her hands.

"Where were you when she was killed?" Raelyn asked in a stern tone, unwilling to let the suspect become distracted.

"I was walking down the street, looking for a place to sleep. That's when I saw people running and heard the screams."

"Did anyone see you?"

Tiv let out an anxious grunt. "I don't know. Someone on the street, probably. Oh! Some Draekalagon deputy guy was yelling at me." She looked down. "I didn't understand what was going on."

Raelyn stood up. "Listen to me. You're going to go to the hospital. Talk to Doctor Myliss. Tell him you want to enroll in the substance abuse withdrawal and recovery program. If he asks you for pay, tell him you'll pay in increments after you are treated. And tell him I said you were good for it."

Tiv stuttered, "I can't afford—"

"After you get out, talk to Eldessia at the antique shop. She's been looking for a strong woman to help her out since her daughter moved off to the Imperium. I'll give you a recommendation."

Tiv's eyes filled with tears. "Why are you helping me?"

Raelyn smiled and nodded. "Because you deserve better than your disease." Raelyn tipped her hat and began to walk out the door.

"The fellows next to me who I found a bother... there were three of them. Three men," Tiv said with a gasp.

Raelyn turned back, eyes narrowed. "Three men?"

"At the booth beside mine." Tiv's fingers slid over the metal surface. "I didn't think much of it. But they were all wearing the same uniform."

"What type of uniform?" Raelyn asked. "Material? Color?"

"I-I don't remember."

Raelyn bowed her head. "Anything helps. Thank you, Tiv."

"Th-thank *you*, Deputy." The suspect-turned-witness wept as Raelyn opened the door.

Deputy Krane stood at the corner of the hallway. "Well, how'd that go?" she asked, her gaze still.

"She didn't do it."

Kasta's cyan eyes rolled over Raelyn. "We already knew that."

Raelyn stopped and crossed her arms. "She also told me that there is a secret substance trade goin' on at Corner Cactus, the saloon where the victim worked. She told me *who* was selling it to her. And she told me three men in uniforms were hangin' around there last night. Before Ella Lane was killed."

Kasta sighed. "Okay, let's hear it."

"Hear what?"

"You got the statement, and I didn't. Give me a by-the-book lawman scolding."

"What are you talking about?" Raelyn looked over her shoulder and lowered her voice. "I want you to go into those other interrogation rooms and do the exact same thing that you just did."

Kasta Krane turned her head, biting her own crooked smirk. "You are full of surprises, Deputy. Full of surprises."

Kasta came in strong again on the next suspect: the farmer. And Raelyn came to the rescue. She had heard of lawmen playing good deputy, bad deputy before. But she had never seen it play out to this effect. Raelyn's sensible and benevolent tone brought out a more talkative side of the suspects. She was on *their* side; and the violent, wrathful deputy from Vulture was not.

Raelyn pulled Kasta off the farmer after only a few seconds. There was no need to give the old man a heart attack. He did not have much information. Plenty of complaints about a competitor who was trying to buy him out of his land, using... questionable means. But that could be reviewed later. The important thing was that the farmer had an alibi. That eliminated two suspects.

The final suspect was the scrap merchant. Raelyn suspected him the most, not because he had any history of medical knowledge or because he exhibited any sadistic traits. But because he was trying to flee town about an hour after the body was found.

As before, Kasta came in with a vengeance. Raelyn "forced" her out of the room. And when Raelyn sat down with an apologetic, welcoming tone, the scrap merchant blurted out everything. He had stolen some scrap from a broken power unit. Unaware that a murder had occurred, and under the impression that the lawmen riding through the streets were after him for petty theft, he fled in a panic.

He informed Raelyn that the scrap was in his carriage and that he would happily return it. The merchant also said that he stopped in Corner Cactus for a drink. His description of the scene checked with Tiv's, except that he did not notice anyone in uniform.

'They must have come in later,' Raelyn thought. 'Closer to the time of Ella Lane's death.'

There was nothing more to learn from inside the walls of the station. It was time to hit the streets.

IV. Corner Cactus

"Men in uniform," said Kasta Krane. "Are there any off-duty Imperial military in town?"

"No." Raelyn walked alongside, across the paved street. "We take note when any Imperial military come through here, believe me."

The rising moons twinkled in Kasta's cyan eyes. "I always thought the killer may be some Imperial with a twisted disdain for Vandeni biology. Some old Imperial sects used to call amphibious traits of the Posaedian Vandeni 'original sin.' And that's what this sicko mutilates: amphibious traits."

Raelyn shook her head. The cool desert air, along with that thought, sent a chill across her skin. "Did they really consider Vandeni traits sinful?"

"Oh yeah," Kasta said with a nod. "It's just a wild theory, and I ain't got no hard evidence for it. It's just something to think about."

"That's wild alright," Raelyn said. "But all theories should be considered."

The dark amethyst night sky swirled overhead. The sidewalks were almost empty, which was rare for this time of night. The tubes of electric light overhead powered the small town of Barren Rock—and guided Raelyn's thoughts. 'All theories are valid, and all questions deserve answers when it comes to detective work.' She stole a glance at Kasta Krane. The young deputy's boots thumped against the wooden walkway. 'Who is the only person in this town that is known to have been near the scene of every Ripper crime?'

'Kasta Krane.' Raelyn answered her own question. 'And she always seems to be following some lead. She's always so *eager* to do things her way. Is she deflecting?' They crossed the street, walking toward the saloon. 'Is she trying to lead the investigation off course? She has had access to the evidence of every Gill Ripper murder.'

A dim light flickered beneath the wooden sign that read "The Corner Cactus Saloon." 'Could Kasta Krane *be* the Gill Ripper?'

Raelyn shook her head as Deputy Krane's excited hand pushed the door open. 'Unlikely. She would have had to ride to Duneland and back to cover her tracks. That's at least a six hour ride each way,' Raelyn thought. 'But all theories are valid.'

The swinging saloon doors opened to reveal a den of silence, save for the droning, gloomy five-count song crackling through the speakers. Darkness flooded the modest establishment. Dim chandeliers shaded with multicolor glass hovered over the tables. Floor lamps with matching multicolor hues lay scattered throughout with no pattern or cohesion. There were only two customers and one bartender—just the man Raelyn wanted to see.

"Oh, Deputy Bovien!" The man's thinly sculpted goatee clung to his smile as he scrubbed a glass. "How can I help you tonight? I've already given two statements." He leaned over the bar, his tall hat casting a shadow over his eyes. "As much as I want to help, I don't think I have the patience to give another."

"I'm not here for an official statement, Mawson." Raelyn stood tall, across from the bartender. He wore a shiny black suit and a ruffled red dress shirt. "I'm here to talk about a few things that may not make you so comfortable."

Kasta leapt atop a stool and sat sideways, leaning over the bar.

He glanced at both women. "And what might that be?"

"The nebula stims, Mawson," Raelyn said. "I know you've got an illegal operation going on here."

"Don't come at me with accusations with no evidence," Mawson said with a sneer. "Don't you have a killer to catch? Get out of my bar."

The bartender began to walk away. Kasta reached over the counter and pulled the man back by his silken lapel. "You're gunna stay right here," she said.

"What? Don't touch me!" he demanded. From the kitchen in the back, a waitress peeked around the corner. "You can't touch me without probable cause. I have rights, little law lady."

Kasta tugged Mawson's bow tie, bringing his face toward hers. "Call me that again, bar boy. I dare you."

Raelyn reached over Kasta's chest and held her back. She maintained steady eye contact with the Vulture deputy, shaking her head. Kasta rolled her eyes and let go of Mawson. Mawson stumbled back and straightened his tie.

"Mister Mawson," Raelyn said, taking a stern tone. "We have a witness who states that you have been selling the proto-nebulous stimulant in this establishment." She held her hands to her hips. "Now, do I need to call in a search team and get the substance-sniffing trugan in here? Or are you going to cooperate?"

Mawson swallowed and looked at the waitress hiding in the shadows. "I'll cooperate," he said. "But I want protection from prosecution."

Raelyn raised her chin. "We'll see."

"Give us what we need for the murder case," Kasta said with an aggressive thrust of her finger. "And no one will care about your stupid stim trade."

Raelyn leaned toward Kasta and whispered, "Deputy Krane, this is not your jurisdiction. You don't have the authority to offer such a deal—"

"You gunna help or not?!" Kasta shouted, ignoring her instruction.

Raelyn bit her lip and cringed. Her eyes crawled up at Mawson for his answer.

"I've already talked to the other lawmen," he said, hands raised. "I'll tell you anything you want. Just please don't take away my bar."

"That's up to you," Kasta said with a smoldering grin.

"Who'd you sell the nebula to last night, Mawson?" Raelyn could not quell the excitement in her voice. She crossed her arms. This bartender knew something. The Ripper was close—behind one last door. And Mawson held the key.

"Pff, I don't remember every customer," Mawson said with an obnoxious giggle. "This stuff is addictive, you know? Lots of people want a taste."

Or not.

Raelyn shook her head. "Who do you remember selling it to?"

Mawson lazily rolled his eyes. His fingernail traced a chink in the wooden bar. "Last night? Umm—that one younger law official..."

"Which one?!" Raelyn's voice rose.

"Look at that," Mawson said with a snide glare. "So offended that one of your own could be a customer. Come on, Deputy. Grow up."

Raelyn took a deep breath, calming herself. 'It's not important right now,' she thought. 'Focus on the case.' "Who else?" she asked, monotone.

"Pff." He tapped his foot against the creaking hardwood floor. A new song, more up-tempo and melodic, began to hiss through the speakers.

"That drifter lady who just got into town a few nights ago. Some of my customers think *she* may be the killer."

"Ha!" Kasta hollered, leaning over the bar. "That's cute."

Mawson sighed. "Can't remember who else. Can I get back to work now? I have customers."

"Not so fast," Raelyn said with a single shake of her head. "Did you by any chance sell to three men? All wearing the same uniform?"

He turned his head, looking to her with a tight squint. "Define 'uniform.'"

"The same outfit. That's all I got to go off."

"Umm, no. But hold on." He looked to the gawking waitress in the back. "Nerry, can you come up here please?"

The waitress crept forward. Her black-and-blue dress danced in the multicolored lighting and flowed through the shadows. "Yes?" she asked, hunched over as she approached.

"Did you see three men in uniform anywhere here last night?" Mawson asked, squeezing the counter. It was as if he thought he could never lose his bar, so long as he did not let go.

"They would have been sitting at one of the tables," Raelyn said, angling her head toward the booths in the back. "Probably that one." She pointed toward the third booth from the entrance, where she assumed the men would have been, based on Tiv's description of the scene.

"Yeah." The waitress nodded, clenching her fist. "Please don't send me to jail. I was only doing what the boss told me."

"Gee. Thanks, Nerry," Mawson said with a long eye roll. "Appreciate the loyalty you have to the business here."

"I'm sorry!" she said. Her lip began to tremble. "It's just... with Ella being killed last night, everything—everything is a mess."

"Tell us about the men in uniforms," Kasta said, tapping her finger on the bar. "And no one goes to jail."

Raelyn's eyes narrowed on Kasta before she rested her gaze on Nerry. "Did they buy any of the substance?"

"No," Nerry said. "They were just ordering rum all night."

"And what kind of uniforms were they?" Raelyn stepped toward the waitress.

"Shipyard uniforms, I think," Nerry said with a nod. "They were black with white cuffs—and umm—white outlines around the pockets."

'Shipyard uniforms,' Raelyn thought. 'That's just great.'

Kasta sat up. "Any chance we can get a look at your digital recordings? See who else walked through here that you may have missed?"

The bartender shrugged. "I'm running an illegal operation here," he said with a scoff. "You really think I'm going to keep a log of visual records?"

Kasta snarled. "I dunno, you've proven pretty stupid so far. Wouldn't surprise me."

"Oh, who the hell even are you?" Mawson's face contorted. "Deputy Bovien, get your pet to settle down."

Kasta spoke through her teeth. "Watch your lip, bar jockey. I have a silver badge that lets me put a cannon bolt through your face—and every word you speak brings me closer to exercising that right."

"Deputy Krane." Raelyn's fist clenched. "Shut your damn mouth." She looked back at the waitress. "That's all we need from you, Nerry. You can go now."

"Please catch whoever killed Ella." Nerry's head sank as she walked back to the kitchen.

"So, we're good, right?" Mawson's brow rose. "I'm protected from any prosecution for my little side business?"

Before Raelyn could answer, Kasta jumped at the chance. "Sure."

"Excellent. Then I'm gunna get back to work." He picked up a bottle of malted whisky and put it on the highest shelf behind the bar. "Thanks for ruining my day, ladies. Now, if you'll excuse me. I need to try to find someone to fill my dead waitress' shift." Mawson stepped to the other side of the bar.

Raelyn treaded toward Kasta. She stood behind the deputy and delivered a sharp whisper. "Stop meddling with Barren Rock law, Krane. Or I'll throw you off this case."

Kasta spun in her stool. "I'd like to see you try."

Raelyn stomped on the metal bar at the foot of the stool, stopping its twist. "You don't have the power to offer side deals to criminals in this town, are we clear?"

"What does it matter? The sale of mind-altering substances is a victimless crime."

Raelyn put her hand on the back of Kasta's chair. "That's not for you to decide." She pointed in the young deputy's face.

"But it is for *you* to do so?" Kasta asked with a smug grin.

"No, it's for the law to do so."

"Oh, damn it all to hell. Are you kidding me?" Kasta groaned and twisted in the stool. "Hey Mawson!" she shouted down the bar. "Yeah, I'm still talking to you. You better never sell nebula or any other illegal stims in this bar again! If you do, I'll ride back down here myself and I'll give you a good talking to with my trugan's jaws and my shock-cannon's barrel."

Mawson shook his head. "I've already invested in a new supply," he moaned.

"Then sell it where it's legal," Kasta retorted.

Mawson looked to the ceiling. "It ain't as profitable where it's legal." His palm smacked his forehead. "But fine, I won't sell in Barren Rock anymore. So long as this won't ever bring me before the law."

"Then we have an understanding," Kasta said with a nod. She looked toward Raelyn. "Happy now?"

Raelyn raised her eyebrows, slack-jawed. "Not happy. But... strangely satisfied, yes."

"I satisfied you?" Her eyelids fluttered and her head shook. "I didn't realize you were capable of satisfaction. This calls for a drink."

"Wait, no, Deputy Krane. We have to regroup and figure out our next move."

"Yeah." Kasta leaned over the bar. "Let's do that here."

"We are not drinking on the job," Raelyn said, stabbing her finger downward.

"Deputy Bovien." Kasta's wry smile annoyed Raelyn more than ever. But this time, it somehow charmed her as well. "The best thing about a case that leads to a saloon is the chance to stop for a drink." She feigned a serious expression. "How do you, in all your expertise in the law, not know this?"

Deputy Raelyn Bovien was silenced.

"Hey, Mawson!" Kasta called out.

Mawson jumped out from under the bar, his eyes darting her way.

"Reach to the top shelf and grab me that fresh bottle of malt whisky, will ya? Pour me a generous glass."

He took cautious steps toward the deputies' end of the bar.

"Don't worry," Kasta said. "I got the platinum for ya. I heard this is an honest business. Happy to support your endeavors." She flashed Raelyn a wink. "Get yourself something too, Deputy. On me."

Raelyn's lips parted, and she let out a shallow breath. "I'll take a whisky too, Mawson," she said, rustling her fingers through her red hair. "Make sure mine is a rye."

The two women of the law sat at the quiet saloon, sipping on their beverages. Raelyn's glass was dripping with condensation, almost full. Kasta's was half empty.

"I thought we'd find a lead here. I really did." Deputy Bovien let out a deep sigh, her elbow on the table and palm to her forehead.

"This guy has given me the bodies of thirteen young women," Kasta said, chewing on a piece of ice. "But no leads. Not one. He doesn't slip up."

Raelyn eyed the young deputy. The dim multicolored lighting outlined her long defined face. "Everyone slips up."

"Not me," Kasta said with a raise of her brow.

"Come on," Raelyn said with a soft groan. "Leave the pride behind until we actually find this guy. If we don't catch up, he's going to kill again. And I'm not letting that happen."

"Okay." Kasta brought her glass against the table with a heavy hand. "We have an advantage here, Deputy. One that I and the other investigators in Vulture never got." She leaned back. "You're in a small town. There's a lot less suspects to pick from than there are in Vulture. The Ripper has put himself in a dangerous spot by killing here. He's grown too arrogant."

"Or too bloodthirsty," Raelyn said.

Kasta shook her head. "I don't follow."

"Think about it." Raelyn sat up straight, her mind aflame with thought. "What if he killed somewhere else because he *couldn't* kill in Vulture? Something was keeping him from going back. But his lust for death was too strong. He had to kill elsewhere."

Kasta reached for her drink. "It's possible." She took a large sip but interrupted herself. "Mm!" Her glass hit the table again as she leaned forward. "What if he's been here for a month? Since the last Vulture murder? Maybe he sensed things getting a little too hot in Vulture? Decided to lay low for a while? But then... a copycat attempts to do his work, and that pisses the Ripper off. So, he has to show him how it's done."

"Could be," Raelyn said with a cautious nod. "But we have screened everyone who has been in town since the last Ripper murder. There's no one who matches up."

"Come on." Kasta's gloved fingers tapped the table. "There has to be someone besides those three suspects you rounded up last night. Someone else that has been through."

"Not that we know of."

"Of course not." Kasta's head sank and her nose crinkled. Her voice sounded deflated. "Knowing the Ripper, he moved in and out without anyone knowing it. He's probably been gone since before the body was found."

Raelyn's brow rose. "Then we follow his trail."

"I do admire your innocent optimism. But the Ripper... he doesn't leave a trail."

"There's a trail," Raelyn said. "There's always a trail." A new song buzzed through the saloon's speakers—anthemic, distorted and multi-instrumental. "Always."

Raelyn's feet tapped to the rhythm. She took a sip of her rye whisky, eying Mawson at the bar. He gawked back. 'Men in uniform,' she thought. 'Shipyard workers.'

She reached into her pocket for her mobile communicator. "Hey, Grig," Raelyn said, holding the device to her ear. "You still in the office?"

"I was actually just leaving." His voice crackled through the device. "Why? What do you want?"

"I need to check if there were any deliveries to the shipyard last night."

Grig's groan came through as feedback. "Fine," he said. "But then I'm going home."

"Thanks, Grig."

"Mhmm."

Kasta squinted. "Deliveries to the shipyard?"

Raelyn leaned toward the Vulture law official, her beige eyes wide. She spoke as fast as her thoughts. "The witnesses saw shipyard workers in here last night. What if the Vulture Gill Ripper isn't a Vulture resident at all?"

Kasta's eyes narrowed further. "What are you getting at?"

"An airship, Krane! What if he has been working on an airship and flying out after his kills? No one questions when a crewman is flying off from city to city." Raelyn's jaw dropped, and she let out a nervous laugh. "He *wanted* everyone to think he was a Vulture resident. But no, Vulture was just his hunting ground."

"Uh-huh," Kasta said, biting her tongue. "Well, it's an interesting theory, but—"

"Deputy Bovien." Grig's voice pierced the speaker of her mobile system.

Raelyn yanked the device to her hear. "Yeah?"

"A cargo ship came in yesterday evening. Dropped off a bunch of orders last night. And today it was loading up on exports. It's set to depart in less than one hour."

Raelyn's and Kasta's eyes locked, both women frozen in silence. The moment was short. The deputies leapt up from the table and made a dash for the door.

"Where's the shipyard?" Kasta shouted from behind as Raelyn pushed the swinging doors of the saloon open.

Raelyn stamped toward the intersection. "Old Town."

"Old Town? The whole town is old."

The harsh, dusty wind fueled Deputy Bovien's steps. She pointed to the southwest. "It's on the other end of Barren Rock, past the industrial avenue."

Kasta caught up, chugging down the rest of Raelyn's rye whisky. "We'll move faster on truganback."

"Then saddle up, city girl."

V. Unknown Cargo

Darkened factories and offices blurred by. Tubes of electricity on each side of the road guided the path of the deputies' trugan as they raced down the industrial avenue. Their violet emergency travel lights warned pedestrians and fellow riders of their relentless gallop.

Raelyn pet Brea's scaled neck. Her steed kept a straight path down the middle of the road. Kasta's trugan raced ahead aggressively. Her emerald-green hide flashed by Brea. The beast unleashed a draconic roar, scaring a slow-moving rider out of her lane.

The cylinders of electric light wrapped around a hexagonal building, interconnecting at the structure's corners. Raelyn and Kasta brought their trugan to a full stop. Raelyn leapt out of the stirrups and ordered Brea to stay. She ran up a flight of tan stairs, her knees absorbing the vibration of their stone. Kasta followed.

Wireless electric hums and mechanical groans reverberated through the high, slanted ceiling. A sleeping woman sat at the front desk.

"The cargo ship!" Raelyn yelled. "What dock is it in?"

The woman licked her lips as she removed her legs from the desk. "Oh—umm—law officials." She yawned. "How can I help you tonight?"

"Bay two!" Kasta yelled, looking at the digital information display on the wall behind them. "Let's go!" She sprinted down the hall.

"Order them to stop their takeoff!" Raelyn stomped her foot, pointing toward the hangar.

"They're already in pre-flight. I can't—"

"By the light of Athenis, never mind!" Raelyn dashed toward Kasta, who had already rounded a corner.

The arches of her feet ached and her sleep-deprived eyes watered. Smells of ozone and electric heat overflowed her nostrils and dripped into her throat. Raelyn came to a halt.

Kasta was shouting at the guard outside of ship bay two.

"Sorry, ma'am. The crew are in pre-flight. No one gets in." The guard blocked the entrance with his wide stance.

"Move now!" Kasta ordered. "My job's more important than yours. So, you're gunna move, or I'll make you sorry."

"Hey, hey," Raleyn said, out of breath. She stood between the arguing parties. "She's with me. We need to apprehend this airship."

"Deputy Bovien! I didn't realize she was with you." The man stepped to the side and extended his hand toward the doorway.

The deputies entered. An old airship hovered over the concrete, dispelling dust clouds toward the hangar walls. Rust and patchwork repairs stained the ship's metallic-white body. The electro-engines shrieked from its tail section as if they struggled to keep the hulking vessel lifted.

"Stop!" Raeyln yelled. There was no answer.

"The loading ramp is down!" Kasta pointed toward the access point extending from the center of the ship's body. The two women ran across the hangar and up the ramp.

Raelyn ducked to enter the ship. The inside of the craft bore a greenish-yellow lighting. The crew looked up from surrounding machinery and digital screens. How could such a large craft manage to feel so... claustrophobic?

Two of the crew members approached quickly, both in black uniforms with white cuffs. One of them said, his voice gruff, "What are you two doing here? We're taking off in a half an hour—"

"We need to talk to your captain," Raelyn interrupted. "Now."

"What's this about?" the other crew member asked. "We don't have time for no local trouble."

Kasta's boots clanked against the metal floor as she walked by them. "Do you have time for a murder?"

A wave of shock halted the two approaching crew members. The other sailors turned toward the two law officials, whispering under the low hum of the machinery.

Raelyn pointed down the narrow corridor. "Take us to the cockpit. Now!"

The men nodded and led them through the halls. The green-yellow lighting flickered.

"Excuse me, Cap?" one of the men said. "Two law officials here. Saying something about a murder."

"And you let them on?" the captain said with a roll of his eyes. "We're already behind schedule, lads. You can't be letting local law on the ship right now."

"Sorry to hold you up there, Captain." Raeyln stepped into the cockpit with a nod. "But we have reason to believe that someone on your ship may be a suspect in the murder last night, here in Barren Rock. And in the Vulture Gill Ripper case."

The captain took off his tall hat and rubbed his forehead, black grease streaking passed his widow's peak. "You can't be serious."

"You can bet we are," Kasta said. "Three men were in Corner Cactus Saloon last night. We need to bring them into the station and have a talk with them."

"We need to talk to *all* of your crew," Raelyn added, an authoritative glare in her eyes.

The pilot turned around, a thick cigarillo between her teeth. "Should I halt takeoff procedures, Cap?"

"No!" the captain shouted, both fists clenched. "I ain't stoppin' my route unless the two of you ladies got a warrant." His nose twitched as he let out a nasally grunt. "We have a small load to drop off in Edge Cliff tomorrow evening, followed by a large load to pick up. Then we gotta get *that* load all the way to Onyx Canyon. So please stop putting me behind schedule and get off my ship."

"A warrant is being processed by the marshal's office of Vulture," Kasta said, crossing her arms. "Either you can cooperate and we'll put you back on your way as soon as possible, or you can deal with the authorities when you land in Edge Cliff. Then you'll have to explain to your superior why you didn't cooperate with the law in Barren Rock when they told you that you may have a killer on board your ship."

The captain stuttered. "Listen, I know my crew. None of them could ever fancy themselves a killer. They be good lads."

"Then let us prove their innocence," Raelyn said. "We'll make sure your superiors know that it's not your fault."

The captain sighed and turned to the younger man next to him, who donned a similar hat. "Round up the lads and ladies," he said. "Tell them to gather in the briefing room on the main deck."

"You shouldn't have done that," Raelyn whispered in Kasta's ear. "When they find out that you don't have a warrant processing in Vulture, they ain't gunna be happy. The shipping company will try to get them to take your badge."

Kasta leaned her way as the crew shuffled into the cramped briefing room. "Well, that won't be a problem if we catch the Ripper," she said with a snicker.

"You better hope we do."

"Lads and lasses," the captain addressed his crew. "These two deputies have boarded our ship. And they seem to believe that one of you may have something to do with a killing that happened at one of the local saloons here."

Gasps and murmurs circulated through the crowd of crew members.

"Now, I know you. You're all good mates. But I do have to cooperate with these officials. So, I would first like to ask—which of the three of ye were at the saloon last night?"

Three hands rose.

"Stand up, please," the captain said.

Three young men stood up, all appearing nervous as they eyed the deputies—and each other.

"We'll talk with you three first, gentlemen," Raelyn said with a slight smile. "Back at the station. But we will need to talk with everyone aboard."

Chatter circulated among the fifteen crew members again. In the crowd, Raelyn felt eyes upon her. Though these eyes only passed for a glance, they burned into her skin, aiming to penetrate her mind. A chill rattled her breath. 'You're here.'

VI. The Trail

The three men from the saloon were eager to cooperate. They gave specific times of their entrance and exit of the establishment. And their alibis checked out with several other crew members, who saw when they returned to the cargo ship.

Deputy Raelyn Bovien scrolled through her data system as they spoke, analyzing the profiles of the crew members. "What do you know about him?" she asked each of the three men who spent time at the saloon.

"Vaun?" one of them said. "We all love Vaun. Nicest guy on the ship. Keeps to himself, mostly. But we don't mind that none."

"Vaun Ahlidius?" the second crewman said, when posed the same question. "He's so friendly. Why? Is he okay?"

When Raelyn asked the third deckhand about him, he said, "I don't know Vaun all that well. But he's always helping everyone with everything. The cooking staff, the loading docks, he even helps the medical officer."

Raelyn jolted at that last mention. "Medical officer? He has medical expertise?"

"Apparently," he said. "Vaun is an airman of many skills."

Raelyn and Kasta brought the captain into the interrogation room. "Vaun Ahlidius is one of the best crewmen I have ever had. He's a bit reserved, but he is a sweet man. Wouldn't harm a soul. So, don't you go accusing him of nothing, ye hear?"

Hours went by. The Barren Rock Marshal's Department sent its law officials in and out of the interrogation rooms. Grig brought cups of coffee to Raelyn and Kasta, who were talking in the hallway.

"Is this all you do here?" Kasta asked, slurping a sip. "Get coffee and sit at the front desk?"

"No. I also track down cargo ships when I want to go home." He bit his lip. "And come back to work in the middle of the night to help with the interrogation of fifteen suspects. All in the name of the badge."

Kasta snapped and pointed at Grig, her fingers in the shape of a pistol. "Keep up the good work."

Grig flashed Raelyn a sardonic smile and stomped away.

"Okay," Kasta said with a sigh. "What's the story with Vaun Ahlidius? Why do you keep asking the crew about him?"

"Read his background report," Raelyn said, rubbing her temples and eyelids.

"I did. Nothing that interesting."

Raelyn reached into her vest pocket for her data system. She handed the device to Kasta. "Look harder."

Kasta rolled her eyes and read aloud. "Born in the High Imperium to a Vandeni mother and Imperial father. Been working in the shipping industry for three years. Blah, blah, blah. Before that, worked in the Imperium as a—a medical examiner. Studied anatomy at... Crescent Peak Lyceum. Wait—" Kasta stammered.

"Read his medical report." Raelyn pointed to the icon on the screen.

Kasta again read aloud. "Healthy, twenty-five-year-old male. Fit for work. Healthy blood tests. Cybernetics: eyesight enhancers, strength multipliers and—no way. It can't be." Her words were stuck in her throat.

Raelyn put her hand on Kasta Krane's shoulder. "Your profile, Krane. He fits your profile."

With a dropping jaw, she brought herself to say the words on the screen. "Cybernetic gill closures."

"An Imperial with a distaste for Vandeni traits—even his own." Raelyn spoke with a grim tone. "And that's not all." She swiped the data system, opening another screen. "He has been on this ship since the first Gill Ripper murders. And I checked the flight records. Every time there was a Ripper murder, this ship was docked in Vulture—and departed within sixty hours of the body being discovered."

Kasta chuckled and nodded, handing the device back to Raelyn Bovien. "Deputy Bovien, we need someone with your skill in Vulture."

Bovien nodded in turn. "It ain't over yet," she said, gulping a drink of coffee. "We still don't have enough for a case against him. Lots of other crew members have been on this ship during the same time frame."

Kasta eyed the interrogation room where he was being kept. "Well, what have we been waiting for, talking to all these other greasy sky sailors? Let's go get a confession. I'll come in strong again! And you can smooth him over."

"Wait a few more minutes, Krane." Raelyn looked around the corner. Several other deputies traded notes. "I have been trying to collect info on this guy from the other crew members—we need all the ammunition we can get."

"Yeah," Kasta said. "And they all seem to think he's so nice and handy."

"Yeah," Raelyn said with a squint. "He's nice. He's got a versatile set of skills. And he's always willing to help." She held up a finger. "But did one crew member—did a single soul on that cargo ship describe Vaun

Ahlidius as a friend? Or even as someone they were deeply acquainted with?"

Kasta's body jolted. Her coffee spilled and splattered over the wooden floor. "No. They didn't." She gasped. "He was hiding something from them."

"He was hiding *himself* from them."

A tone rang from Raelyn's communications device. As she answered, Kasta looked on, confused. "Cretaeith, talk to me." She put the call on conference mode so that Kasta could hear.

A Draekalagon of Oglund, Deputy Cretaeith hissed into Raelyn's ear, "I am in Ahlidius' cabin. And I found some items that you're not gunna believe, Raelyn."

"Talk to me."

"A black cloak, hung in the back of his closet, hidden between his work uniforms and casual wear."

Raelyn squinted. "What else?"

The lawman responded with a reptilian chuckle. "A very tall black hat to go with it." He cleared his throat. "But it gets even wilder. He has surgical equipment under his mattress. And—get ready for this—printed clippings of the Vulture Gill Ripper headlines."

Raelyn laughed, but was swift to bury her excitement. "Deputy Cretaeith, get all those items into evidence and start working on your report."

"The whole lot is already on its way to evidence, Deputy Bovien." The transmission disconnected.

Kasta took a step back. "It's him, isn't it? It really is him."

"Now we can get in there," Raelyn said, putting her communication device away.

"Okay," Kasta said with a deep breath. "What's our angle?"

Raelyn nodded. "We'll do it like last time. You come in heavy and I'll pull you back. But don't go *too* strong this time. He's not going to crack easily, and I want us both in there the entire time. We'll record the conversation for the courts. So, try to keep it by the book here, Krane."

She looked to Raelyn with a slight smile. They walked side-by-side down the hallway, toward the interrogation room. "I'll follow your lead," Kasta said with a wink.

Outside the door, Raelyn checked her data system to confirm that the digital recording devices in the interrogation room were active. She stole a glance through the circular glass window to see a lanky man sitting at the table with his fingers interlocked. Raelyn took one last look at Kasta, flashing her a nod. The young Vulture deputy nodded back, and Raelyn opened the door.

"Deputies!" the man said. His gleaming smile stretched across his long face. "I thought that you two may be here soon."

Raelyn squinted as she closed the door. "Did someone tell you we were coming?"

"No, no." His smile held its place as he spoke, and it made Raelyn feel sick. "I just did not think that the last deputies asked very astute questions. And I figured that the two lead investigators would like a word with me." His Imperial accent was strong. Too strong—exaggerated past the point of being natural.

Kasta stepped forward, her thumbs in her belt. "How did you figure we would be fixin' to talk to you in particular, Ahlidius?"

"Oh well, logic dictates it." His long skeletal fingers separated, and he sat up straight. His unnerving smile refused to leave his grey face. "You have deemed that someone on the ship on which I humbly serve may be a suspect in those horrible murders."

Those bony fingers cracked as they fell to the table, one by one. And that smile made a sudden reversal, becoming a steep frown. "Now, I would hate to see a case against any of my fellow crew members—and I truly doubt any of them could be capable of such terrible crimes." He looked down, taking a short breath. "But I will aid the law in whatever way I can." His pale white eyes swiveled back and forth between Kasta and Raelyn. "Justice is the most important virtue to us all on this night."

"I would agree," Kasta said, her expression as neutral as the white table.

"Well, I'm happy that you are eager to help, Vaun." Raelyn forced a smile and gestured toward the suspect with her data system. "You don't mind if I call you Vaun, do you?"

"No, please do!" Vaun said, his pointed chin angled low. "They say we have a propensity for the formal in the Imperium." A low chuckle slipped between his words, and his angular face turned sideways. "But it's lost on me."

An image flashed in Raelyn's mind of red streaks splattering onto Vaun's grinning face, of his long fingers reaching into the necks of young women, and of him tearing apart the body of Ella Lane. Raelyn forced the image deep within her mind and chuckled with the suspect.

She sat across from him and placed her data system on the table. "So, Vaun." She leaned back as Kasta paced behind her. "Give us some insight. Tell us if there's anyone aboard your ship that you suspect."

Vaun sat up, his tall frame bringing his face into shadow. "Well, I actually have followed this case closely."

"Oh yeah, we know," Kasta said, still pacing.

"Krane!" Raelyn said with a strike of her hand and shake of her head. Vaun looked at the women in confusion. Was it real or fake confusion?

"We conducted searches of everyone's cabin on board the vessel, Vaun." Raelyn leaned forward. "Standard procedure when something like this happens."

"Ah, I figured as much," Vaun said with a nod. "So, you found my news clippings? Yes, I have developed a bit of a fascination with the case of the Vulture Gill Ripper." He looked to Kasta through his long black eyelashes. "I know much of you, Deputy Krane. I have seen your name mentioned in the news articles. You're not quite how I pictured you..."

"That's funny," Kasta said with a tight purse of her lips. "You're exactly how I pictured you."

Raelyn groaned and shook her head as Vaun's eyes narrowed. "Please forgive my colleague's suspicion," Raelyn said with a bow of her head. She forced herself to keep eye contact with him. "She's been on this investigation for quite some time."

"Oh, my. I *do* understand." Vaun's wide smile returned, more slanted this time. "This must be a frustrating case for you, Deputy Krane. To have the Ripper get away from your grasp so many times. I cannot imagine the distress that must cause you—always being one step behind."

Raelyn cleared her throat, her gaze crawling toward Kasta. 'Please don't lash out,' Raelyn thought. 'Not yet.'

"Not as much distress as this butcher's victims," Kasta said, standing tall behind Raelyn with her arms crossed. "Or their families. Losing their daughters and sisters and wives because of some *unmethodical* slasher with a sick fetish."

Vaun swallowed and froze. His fingernail scratched the surface of the table. "I don't know if we can call the Ripper unmethodical," he said with a titter. "I think there is a little more to this particular individual than meets the eye."

'That a girl, Kasta,' Raelyn thought. 'You found a chink in his ego. I'll exploit it. And you find another.'

"What do you think about him?" Raelyn rested her elbow on the back of the chair. "Is there a method to his madness? What's he trying to say?"

Vaun Ahlidius leaned forward, his finger stretched toward the ceiling. "Well, I think you have misappropriated the sex of the Ripper." He smacked his lips together. "You should be looking for a woman."

Raelyn's lips twisted. "A woman? And why is that?"

"Consider the facts, Deputies." He leaned back, steepling his fingers. "Only a woman could have the trust of another woman in those dark alleys of Vulture. It would take a woman to have access to the... *victims* when they are in such vulnerable positions. And a woman would have the motive to kill these attractive ladies who flaunt themselves so lustfully."

Kasta let out a dry cackle. Her boots squeaked on the floor as she shuffled her foot.

Raelyn gave the mixblood man a sideways glance. "'Flaunt themselves.' Vaun, what do you mean?"

"Oh, these murders. They are clearly crimes of jealousy." He laughed, and Raelyn again saw a flash of blood on his face. "Have you not considered this, Deputy Krane?"

Kasta leaned on the table. "No. And I think that theory sounds about as ridiculous to you as it does to me."

Raelyn leaned toward her. "Deputy Krane, step back." She pretended to mouth words of caution to the young Vulture law official. "Vaun, she doesn't speak for Barren Rock. I find that theory quite interesting. You developed such a theory just from reading the articles about the case?"

"I did." Vaun's polished white teeth crept through his tight smile. "And there are only four women who serve aboard our ship." He nodded and snickered, running his fingers through his slicked-back hair. "So that should help you narrow it down."

The room was silent, save for the hum of the dim light above. Vaun Ahlidius was deflecting, and it was time to put him back on the trail—the trail of blood that led to him. "Do you think the killer has any kind of background in the field of surgery—or medicine?" Raelyn asked.

Vaun shook his head. "No, I don't think that would be necessary."

"I don't know," Raelyn said with a sigh. "To be able to so thoroughly extract a respiratory system. It's not easy to perfectly dissect and fillet a set of gills and every connected capillary." She bit her tongue before speaking her next words, but she had to do so. "It's... almost impressive, isn't it?"

Vaun's gangling torso crept Raelyn's way. "I find it impressive too. But knowledge of surgery would not be required." He shrugged. "Though I suppose it would help."

"I imagine it would help a lot," Raelyn said. "But you would know more than I would, with your experience in anatomy and education in medicine."

"Ah, so you've done some research into my past career." Vaun spoke slowly, with a snarl under his voice. "I would hope that does not give you an inclination to think I had something to do with the Ripper case."

"No, no." Raelyn shook her head. "Of course not. I just was wondering if you could guide us with your expertise on the subject. How much would the Ripper have to know of Vandeni anatomy?"

Kasta rested her back and foot against the wall, half-hidden in shadow.

"Well," Vaun said. "It would require dedication more than anything."

"Dedication?" Raelyn's brow rose.

"Yes," Vaun said. "Dedication to choose a proper target, to conduct the execution and complete his delicate work in silence. To return to shadows unseen, a watcher in the dark."

"*His*," Kasta hissed. Her cyan eyes locked onto Vaun. "Didn't you say that you had it in your head that the killer was a woman?"

"I did," Vaun said with an enigmatic smile. "But you have convinced me otherwise, Deputy Krane." His pointed chin tucked in. "It is a privilege to see such aptitude from a deputy detective up close. Especially one as beautiful and young as you."

Magmatic anger steamed from Kasta's tightened fist.

"What made you decide to stop studying anatomy?" Raelyn blurted, hoping to distract her fellow deputy before she said something rash. "You must have been making more money working in the High Imperium as a medical examiner than you do working on cargo ships for Cloud Compass Trading Company."

"Oh, the money was never all that important to me." Vaun's rigid posture broke as he rested his fingers over his waist. "I just... desired a change of scenery, and I had always aspired to travel." He chuckled. "I figured I may as well get paid to do so rather than dip into my own bank accounts."

As Raelyn laughed with him, Kasta stepped forward—her boot thumped against the edge of the table, and she left it resting there. "Yet, of all the opportunities in shipping and transportation, you chose to work as a deckhand for Cloud Compass. A low-profit company that sends out its cargo using airships that are older than me."

Vaun sneered and tried to interject, but Kasta spoke over him. "You could have worked for Continental Cargo or Sky and Seas, one of the big shipping companies. And you could have worked as a medical officer, making double the platinum you are now." Kasta paused, leaning over the table. "And you could have seen a lot more of the world if that was truly your goal."

"I respect your drive and determination, Deputy Krane." Vaun's lips pressed together, and his spine straightened. "But you have taken this conversation in an unpleasant direction. And if it continues this way, I shall end it."

"You don't get to decide—"

"Krane!" Raelyn shouted and slammed her fist on the table. "Stop taking this tone with our witness. You are out of line. If you continue taking this tone, I will make you wait in the hallway."

Kasta removed her foot from the table and drew a deep sigh. "Whatever."

"Vaun," Raelyn said, hands raised. "I appreciate all the information you have given us thus far." With a slow nod, she said, "I mean that. Thank you." She almost gagged on her own words.

"As I said," Vaun said with a smile. "I am happy to aid the law by any means possible." He took a deep breath, and his eyes sparkled with his pearly smile. "This Ripper investigation has gone on too long, and if I can help the two of you close the case, I am proud to do so."

Raelyn picked up her data system. "Okay, Vaun. As is part of the procedure with every crew member from your vessel, we need to clear your name." She looked deep into his eyes. "Think you can help us do that?"

"I would be delighted!"

"Okay," Raelyn said. "I know you said you were interested in the Ripper case, but why keep paper printouts of the news articles? I don't know anyone who reads their news from a paper. Wouldn't it be easier to just store them on a data system?"

"Oh, yes," Vaun said. "It would be, but I have a... fondness for the old-fashioned."

"So why hide them under your mattress?"

He shrugged. "Well, I didn't want to scare the crew."

"Makes sense," Raelyn said. 'That makes absolutely no sense,' Raelyn thought.

Kasta stepped toward the table, her eyes fluttering back and forth between Raelyn's data system and Vaun.

"And what about—"

"The surgical equipment," Vaun said, his brow arching over his long forehead. "I figured that you must have found my case of surgical equipment if you found my news clips." He leaned back in the chair. "As you previously stated, I used to study anatomy. And I worked as a medical examiner."

"So, why keep them? You're not in medicine anymore."

"Well," he said. "I like to keep a collection of my things—mementos if you will."

"Keep any organs of young women as mementos?" Kasta said, a harsh strain in her voice.

"Your tone, Krane!" Raelyn's words thundered through the small room. "You're out of line."

Vaun shot back and gasped. "Deputy Krane, that is a disgusting allegation. I would never even think to keep the organs of young girls. The very thought sickens me."

His attention returned to Raelyn, and his tone turned light again. "On the topic of my surgical tools, Deputy Bovien, there is further reason for my keeping them. I suppose I like to think that I would be able to help the medical officer if there were ever an emergency aboard the ship. I would hope my surgical skills could come in handy in such an event." With an elated sigh, he added, "'Vigilance is a virtue,' my father always used to say."

"And the black outfit hidden in your closet?" Raelyn asked. "What's that for?"

"Oh, in the event of special occasions," Vaun said. "You never know when a banquet could be called for."

Kasta's finger tapped the handle of her pistol. "Between the cloak and that tall hat, you could get around unrecognized." Her piercing gaze contrasted with her half grin. "And with that camouflageable Imperial skin you have, you'd be able to blend in with the shadows in the cover of night."

"Ask my fellow crew members, Deputy Krane," Vaun said, drumming his steepled fingers from pinky to pointer. "I guarantee that they have never seen me wearing it while exiting the ship."

'That makes it even stranger,' Raelyn thought. 'Time to get a bit more aggressive here.' "Vaun, I have to ask." She pointed toward his neck. "What's the story with your gills? Why cybernetically seal them?"

Vaun's face drooped low as he reached for his neck, feeling the metal panels and outlined scar tissue that sealed what once were two gills on each side of his neck. "Oh." A grin overtook his face in a jarring instant. "I was born with a condition. My gills were very easily prone to infection, especially in the wintry weather of the Imperial mountains." His head tilted sideways. "Unfortunately, it's a condition not uncommon to mixbloods. I decided to seal them rather than deal with the recurring spells of illness."

Kasta squinted an eye, nodding upward. "They have procedures to augment the tissue of the bronchia, to make them less susceptible to contamination." She shrugged. "Why not just do that? Probably a lot cheaper. And less painful as well."

'Thank the stars that Kasta is here,' Raelyn thought. 'I didn't even know about such procedures.'

"That was not an option for me. My doctor and I determined that the remove-and-seal procedure was best." He spoke through a grumbled laugh. "Plus, I'm not much of a swimmer anyway."

'This guy has an answer for everything, doesn't he?' The thought made Raelyn want to roll her eyes. But she refrained. 'Okay. Let's hit him with some rapid fire.'

"What about your eyes?" Raelyn said with a tight glare. "Your birth documentation states that your eyes were green at birth. Now they are pale white? Why change your eye color, Vaun?"

"Well," Vaun said. "I just never thought my green eyes suited my grey skin." He let out a titter. "I wanted my father's eyes.

"Your *Imperial* father," Kasta said, reaching into her jacket pocket. She pulled out a cigarillo.

"And your lips." Raelyn spoke fast and with punctual inflection. "Is that *lipstick* you're wearing, Vaun?"

"Yes," he said. "Is wearing lipstick a crime?"

"No, of course not. And I'm sure you have another layer of grey tattooed beneath." Kasta lit her cigarillo. "But why are you trying so hard to hide your Vandeni traits? Are you embarrassed by them?"

Raelyn sat up, straight and stiff. "Ashamed, maybe?"

Vaun's hands slapped the table, and his long fingers rapped over the surface. "This is beginning to feel like an interrogation. And if that is the case, I shall need to call legal counsel for representation."

"Why do you feel like you're being interrogated, Ahlidius?" Kasta blew out a cloud of smoke as she stepped toward him, her glove dragging over the table. "We just want to pick your brain a bit." She paused. "Don't you wanna help the law? In whatever way you can?"

"Please don't smoke in here," he said.

"Cooperation is key here, Vaun." Raelyn's words were calm, but her nerves trembled. Vaun sank in his chair, and his teeth rattled. Was he bending? Or breaking? Or was his true self emerging? Raelyn's right hand gripped her pistol.

"I have cooperated with you," Vaun said with a snarl. "Now if you'll excuse me, I would like to get back to my crew." He shot up from his chair, and his long frame cast a thin shadow over Raelyn.

"Sit the hell down!" Kasta barked. She reached for her pistol as well, making sure Vaun could see it. "You are not to walk out of here until we give you permission."

"Whoa, whoa," Raelyn said. "Let's all settle down here."

"I will be reporting you both to your superiors," Vaun said. He stared Kasta down.

"Report us to your legal counsel." Kasta blew a stream of smoke up into the man's face. "They are the only ones who are going to care what you have to say for the rest of your life."

Vaun's figure towered over Kasta, but she was unfazed. "Please do not smoke in here," he reiterated.

"How about I do whatever I want and there's nothing you can do about it?" Kasta stepped his way, ashing her cigarillo at his feet. "How does that make you feel, Gill Ripper?"

Raeyln surged to her feet. "Stop with the accusations, Krane. This is not the time or place."

"Put an end to these games!" Vaun shouted, clenching both of his fists. "Do you think I am ignorant to your ploy, Deputy Bovien?"

Kasta took another step toward him, batting her eyelashes.

Raelyn cleared her throat. "Of course not, Vaun. You're a very intelligent man—"

"Then get her away from me," Vaun muttered.

"Or what?" Kasta said, then pursed her purple lips. "What are you going to do if Deputy Bovien lets me stay *right* here?"

'Is she doing what I think she is doing?' Raelyn was careful to remove her pistol from its holster. 'Dangerous game, you're playing here, Krane. But it's working.' An idea came to bloom. Could it work? Could it be just what they needed to push him over the edge?

It was worth a shot. Raelyn got Kasta's attention with a subtle upward nod and pointed to her neck.

Kasta read Raelyn's body language and nodded back. After flashing a smirk Vaun's way, she released a long drag of her cigarillo. Through her gills.

Vaun's teeth sank into his artificial grey lips. "Don't do that again," he whispered.

"Do what?" Kasta asked in a high-pitched voice, releasing another stream of smoke through the three gills on each side of her neck.

"Flaunt yourself. It's shameful."

"I have nothing to be ashamed of, Vaun," Kasta said. She went for another drag. "The shame is all yours."

Vaun crept toward Kasta, staring her down with his cold white eyes. "You will *stop* flaunting your original sin at me, you despicable little fish-girl."

Raelyn drew her pistol and began to take aim. But Kasta flashed a shake of her head as Vaun backed her down.

"Original sin, huh?" Kasta cleared her throat and again took a drag from her cigarillo. "What makes you such an expert?"

"I am doing the Guardians' work, Kasta Krane." His eyes stretched wide and refused to blink. "I am the chosen warrior of the divine, sent to rid the world of its impurities."

Raelyn thought about intervening, but Kasta remained determined and unflinching. "And just how do you do that?"

"Would you like to know? You spiteful, loose-lipped little streetwalker." He placed his arm on the wall, trapping Kasta. His face overhung hers. "When I get out of here, I will be sure to show you."

"No, you won't," Raelyn said, aiming her pistol at him. "Vaun Ahlidius. In the name of the Barren Rock Marshal's Department, you are under arrest for the murder of Ella Lane."

"You have no proof," Vaun said, his chin elevated. "Your case is an embarrassment."

"We have enough evidence to take you to trial." She extended her arm; her silver pistol trembled with her hand. "Step away from Deputy Krane, and we'll get you booked. Then you can call a legal counselor to discuss your options."

Vaun grunted. "This is an atrocity of justice! I'm a respected member of—ahhhhhhhg!" Vaun's body lit up in an eruption of electricity. His gangling arms snapped upward. Convulsing and groaning, he fell to the ground. Raelyn's jaw dropped. The final streams of electric blue fizzled away, and smoke arose from his still body.

Raelyn put her hand over her mouth. "Oh my—damn it, Krane, what did you do?"

Kasta shrugged. "You try having this psycho hovering over you for that long." She cringed and shook her head. "Unsettling to say the least."

Raelyn took off her hat and let out a deep breath. "Please tell me that you had your weapon set to incapacitate."

"Ok yeah, obviously." Kasta pointed to the lethality toggle on her shock-cannon. "We didn't just do all that work so I could kill the bastard." She gave her pistol a couple of twirls and slid it back into her holster. "Vaun Ahlidius, Vulture *also* is placing you under arrest for the murders of Fethalia Depsey, Freyis Pel, Alva—

"Krane, Krane," Raelyn interrupted. "He can't hear you—he's knocked out cold." She gestured to Vaun's motionless body.

Kasta paused with a curl of her upper lip. "I know. It's for the digital logs," she said, motioning toward the recording device in the corner.

"Oh, umm—" Raelyn's eyebrows rose as she sought the proper words. "Okay. I guess."

"Not to mention," Kasta said, her chest jutting out. "You said it with such a fiery passion. So, I wanted to do it too."

Raelyn shook her head. And her heavy eyes shut for a long blink. "Carry on."

"Alva Clayson, Corrie Emith..."

VII. In the Name of the Badge

"Raelyn, Deputy Krane."

Both deputies jumped as Grig opened the door to Raelyn Bovien's office.

"Yeah, what is it, Grig?" Raelyn asked with an unflattering rasp in her voice.

"Marshal Zeller has Marshal Jos via transmission. They wanna talk to the both of ya."

"Holy hell." Kasta raised her head from Raelyn's desk, her hair a frizzy black mess. "What time is it? What day is it?"

"Just past daybreak," Grig said. "You guys dozed off about an hour ago. Maybe two."

Kasta squinted at him. "Do *you* ever sleep?"

"Not since you came to town, Deputy Krane." He slammed the door.

"I don't think he likes me," Kasta said with a heavy cough.

"He's moody," Raelyn said, stretching her arms wide. "But a good guy once you get to know him."

"Should we get in there?" Kasta asked, forcing herself to stand up.

"Ready if you are."

"So, let me get this straight." Marshal Zeller's bushy white mustache followed his scowl. "You shot the suspect?"

"No, no." Raelyn sighed, sitting up as straight as she could in her chair. "I had my sights on him, but I didn't fire." She pointed toward the young Vulture deputy whom she had spent the last day with. "Kasta did."

"Well that makes more sense." Jos' hoarse laugh crackled through the speaker.

"Suspect was getting hostile," Kasta said with a tight smile and a quick shrug. "I felt threatened. So, I put him down and out." She winked at Zeller. "But not permanently."

"I'll have to review the recordings." Zeller grunted and smacked his lips. "Deputy Bovien, how in the hell did you develop such a spot-on profile for this madman in the span of a day?"

"Oh, it wasn't my profile." Raelyn extended her hand toward Kasta. "It was Deputy Krane's. Once we had the crewman from the ship in custody, I just connected the dots."

"Hot damn. You were right all along, Kas." Marshal Jos' pride emanated from his words. "I told you she can get the job done, Deputy Bovien."

"I was wrong to underestimate either of you," Raelyn said with a thin smile. "Couldn't have done it without her."

Kasta stood with a guarded stance. But she looked to Raelyn with an assured nod.

"I trust I will find all this in your official report, Deputy Bovien." Zeller leaned back. His wrinkled brow creased tight. "But how did you even figure out that he was on that airship?"

"Everything else was just good old detective work, Marshals." She clasped her hands. "We talked to the suspects that had previously been apprehended, cleared their names and got some valuable information.

We theorized that the culprit may have been slipping in and out of town after every murder, using employment on an airship to cover his tracks. Thus, creating the *illusion* that he was a Vulture resident."

She shrugged. "So, we checked the cargo port records. And what do ya know: one cargo ship had come through town since the time of the murder. And it was still docked."

Kasta grasped her elbow, pointing toward Raelyn. "What she said."

"Wow," Marshal Zeller said. "I look forward to reading more about this in your report."

Raelyn shut her eyes and nodded.

Jos' voice came through the speaker on Zeller's desk. "You'll be delighted to know that the case against Vaun Ahlidius is even more damning than we thought."

"How so?" Raelyn asked, leaning toward the desk.

"Well, I have put out digital scans of his face to every Marshal Department in Vanda. And later, I'm going to contact some military headquarters in the Imperium as well." He paused, and Raelyn eyed the communication device with rapid nods of impatience. "Anyway, not many of the departments have gotten back to me yet. But Edge Cliff did. And they have a witness who gave a description of a man who tried to drag her under a tunnel at knifepoint."

Kasta's jaw dropped. "No... way!"

"You betchya, Kas. Vaun's distinctive features definitely are not going to play to his advantage in court." He cleared his throat. "That's not all. She said he was wearing a black top hat and a black cloak."

Raelyn laughed and brought her gloved hands together for a single clap. "This is excellent news. The case was already pretty strong. But now it's surefire. There's no way he wins now. He'll be in prison for life."

Marshal Jos cleared his throat. "And don't be shocked if more reports start flowing in. If it turns out he killed someone in a death penalty territory, being in for life may not even be on the table." Someone shouted in the background on the transmission. "Listen, I gotta run. Excellent work, Deputies." His voice sharpened. "Kas, be sure you get *me* a report. Get to work on that as soon as you're back in Vulture."

"Yeah." Kasta grinned. "I'll have a cadet get to work on a report as soon as I get back to Vulture."

"Gunna pretend I didn't hear that." Marshal Jos disconnected the transmission.

"Okay." Marshal Zeller's leather chair squeaked as he slouched over his desk. "It looks like you two have built a really solid case. We'll decide where to go as far as further charges after I read your report, Deputy Bovien."

"Yes, I'll get you all the facts." She nodded, and Zeller gave her a cold stare. Did her annoyance seep through her voice?

"Grig," Marshal Zeller said after tapping on his data system. "Can you send Deputy Colverg in here?"

Marshal Zeller's hands rested on his bulging belly. "Now, I don't want to take anything away from the good work you just did in the name of the law. For both this department and Vulture. But Colverg had some pretty disturbing things to say to me when I walked into the station this morning."

"Colverg." Kasta's head tilted and her eyes narrowed. "Who is Colverg?" With a muted snap, she pointed to Raelyn. "Oh, he means the idiot!"

On cue, Deputy Colverg marched into the office. His snakeskin boots clacked against the hard floor. "Hello, ladies," he said with a smile. "I have some interesting information from some of our dearest citizens stating that the two of you have been acting all out of sorts. Threatening citizens without cause. Offering deals that you have no business offering to potential offenders of Barren Rock law. Intimidating suspects who are under the protection of this great department. Lying about warrants being processed in other cities?" He stepped to the other side of the room and leaned forward, resting his hand on Marshal Zeller's desk. "Now I don't think this is the type of conduct that we like to aspire to in Barren Rock, is it, Marshal Zeller?"

Zeller's face contorted as he scooted his chair away from Deputy Colverg.

"Lemme get this straight." Kasta leaned against the wall with her arms crossed, her black hat blocking her eyes. "Deputy Bovien and I have been up all night, trying to catch a sadistic murderer." She looked to Zeller. "And succeeding, mind you," she said with a bite. Her shadowy gaze returned to Colverg. "And you have been using that same time to try to *tell* on us?"

Colverg scoffed and spoke with a titter. "Now wait just a minute."

"Deputy Colverg." Marshal Zeller's glacial voice rose in volume with every syllable of the name he spoke. "Wait outside."

Colverg looked to the marshal. "B-but I have more information—"

"You have supplied the necessary information. So please, step outside and I shall do whatever I see fit with said information."

Colverg continued to stutter. "But why?"

"Because my badge is gold and yours is silver!" Zeller growled. "And if you speak another word before stepping out of this office, we can go ahead and make it copper."

Colverg paused, rolled his eyes and trudged out the door.

Marshal Zeller took a deep breath. "Anyway, I apologize that the two of you had to see that."

Kasta could not hold back laughter. And the sight of Kasta bursting with joy forced a giggle out of Raelyn.

But she bit her lip when Zeller continued speaking. "I'm not one to cozy up to Deputy Colverg. But he's an honest law official. And these accusations are no laughing matter. Trust between lawman and civilian is a cherished component of Barren Rock life." He sighed through his nose. "So, do I have to open an investigation into the matter of your conduct?" He paused, his eyes homing in on Raelyn. "Did you commit any of these violations which Deputy Colverg so fervently claims you did?"

Raelyn's lips separated to reply, but Kasta spoke louder and faster. "It was all me," the Vulture deputy said with a shrug. "I don't utilize conventional methods of detective work. Or of enforcing the law in general."

An enigmatic smile shone across her youthful face. She tipped her hat upward. "Deputy Bovien has been attempting to reel me in the entire time." Her head tilted back and forth. "With... mixed success. I know I'm a bit headstrong. But let me just say: If I didn't have her out there with me, you'd be hearing *a lot* more complaints about conduct or whatever."

Marshal Zeller smacked his lips and dipped his head. "Okay," he said. "Well, I can't discipline you, since you are not one of my deputies." He stabbed his finger her way. "But I am going to report your misconduct to Marshal Jos. And he can discipline you in whatever way he sees fit."

"If that makes you feel better about yourself, old-timer, you go right on ahead." Kasta tipped her hat and turned toward the exit. "Now if the two of y'all would excuse me, it's a long way back to Vulture. Been a pleasure." She nodded at Raelyn before yanking the door shut.

"A handful, isn't she?" Marshal Zeller leaned back. His tan boots thumped over his desk.

"Yes," Raelyn said with a slow nod. "To say the least."

"Listen," Zeller said. "You've done some real good work here. It ain't easy to have to work with a maverick like that. Especially one who you don't know. But you did the work and got the job done. I'm proud to have you in this department."

Raelyn nodded. "I'm proud to be here, sir."

"That's good." He leaned forward and reached for his mobile system. "Okay, I gotta make some calls. You get me that report as soon as you can." His finger thrust toward her. "But not until you get some rest."

"Yessir," she said. She stood and strutted toward the door but turned around. "Hey, Marshal," she said with an eager tone. "Please don't go too hard on Deputy Krane when you report her behavior during the investigation to Marshal Jos. She may not carry herself with the dignity that you'd expect from a Vandeni law official, but she's a good deputy. And I meant what I said: I couldn't have done it without her."

A slight smile inched up the side of Zeller's face. "I'll keep that in mind."

VIII. The Wake of Justice

The early morning rays of Athenis reached for the streets of Barren Rock. Her streams of blue offered light, life and warmth to the town, uninterrupted by clouds or breeze. Citizens rode through the streets on their trugan and walked down the wooden sidewalks. The low purr of chatter and slow gallop of the trugan put a smile on Raelyn's face.

"Hey," she called out to Kasta Krane. The young woman in black leaned against the railing of the stairway, puffing on a cigarillo. "Got an extra one of those for me?"

"For the master madame of the interrogation room?" Kasta turned her way. "Absolutely." She reached into her pocket.

The power tubes buzzed overhead, carrying endless spirals of electricity to the marshal's department and the rest of the city. Raelyn took a long drag as Kasta lit the dark cigarillo. "You know, you didn't have to cover for me, Krane." Raelyn looked up at her, her beige eyes holding an acute glare.

"I didn't. I just told the truth. I took some... improvisational liberties regarding protocol. And you were trying to level me out."

"Improvisational liberties." Raelyn raised an eyebrow. "I like that. Think it would hold up in court?"

Kasta's head tilted as she raised her cigarillo. "I dunno. Give it a shot and tell me how it goes."

Raelyn's expression flattened. "But in all seriousness, you were my responsibility here. And I did not stop you from conducting things your way. Hell, I encouraged it at times." She shook her head. "You shouldn't have to face all the consequences—"

"Deputy." Kasta Krane placed her hand on Raelyn's shoulder. "You got a hell of a future waiting for you in the law. Don't be sorry for not laying it on the line for me. You did what you had to do."

Deputy Bovien laughed. "The law is lucky to have you as well, Deputy Krane."

Kasta shrugged. The two women exchanged a firm handshake. They walked down the stairs, and Kasta called her trugan over. "That's right, Kai," she said with a warm tone. "We're ridin' on back east."

Raelyn took a short drag from her cigarillo. "You're riding all the way back to Vulture?"

"Eventually," Kasta said as she climbed atop her saddle. Her trugan released a soft growl. "That's the thing about the Vanden desert." She leaned forward, looking off into the distance. "Sometimes it just... leads you where it pleases."

Raelyn spoke through a quiet laugh. "Well, call us in if you ever need aid." She nodded and crossed her arms. "Barren Rock and Vulture have always been cross-continent partners. And I think that you and I have strengthened that relationship today."

Kasta's cyan eyes tightened. "Cut the fancy talk, Deputy. I'm calling you down to Vulture if I ever have a stubborn suspect who won't crack. And I'll buy you another whisky. Maybe you'll even get a chance to finish it this time."

Kasta's smug, crooked grin overtook the left side of her face. But it did not irritate Raelyn. It made her smile in turn. "I can only hope, Deputy Krane."

"Call me Kasta."

"Call me Raelyn."

Kasta shook her head and took hold of her reins. "I don't wanna," she said with a playful shake of her head. The young woman in black rode forward and turned down the main street. Raelyn watched as her silhouette faded into the tremoring blue glow of Barren Rock.

Deputy Raelyn Bovien turned around and took a long look at the marshal's office. She took a drag from the bitter cigarillo and stepped away from the building, making her way down the wooden sidewalk. For the first time in three nights, she was going to sleep in a bed.

OF DUELS AND DEBTS

"You're using loaded dice."

Two card players looked up. Their eyes met. One flashed the dealer a shrug.

Nellik of Grathank hissed another accusation. "Your dice rolls have beat my cards too many times. What's your angle, swindler?" Nellik's tongue flicked, tasting the thick, smoky air.

One player's head slanted sideways. His blue-grey Vandeni hand grabbed hold of the dice. "Guess I just got the hot hand tonight."

Nellik's clawed fingers wrapped around a handful of platinum coins. "It'll be cold when I'm done with it." He tossed the coins across the table. They clinked in front of the dealer.

"I think you've played enough tonight, Nellik," a crackling voice uttered over a chorus of belligerent laughter, slurred chatter and pitchy singing. A hand clutched Nellik's wide shoulder. His scaled skin tightened.

Nellik pivoted in his chair to see a man in a lizard-skin mask. The man's eyes glowed an unnatural green. "I'll decide when I've played enough, Breylu." Nellik's pupils narrowed into thin vertical slits. "And I'll have played enough when either I win back my coin or I catch this *swindler* in the act." His long claw pointed toward the nearest opposing player.

The opponent responded with a mocking laugh.

"Nellik," Breylu said with a bite, his grip on his shoulder tightening. "You've played enough."

"Come on." Nellik growled, then smirked. "Just one more hand, boss."

The amphibious Breylu and reptilian Nellik locked eyes, their dead stare unbroken by a shattering glass at a nearby table. "Okay," Breylu said. He released his grip from the Draekalagon's shoulder and lifted a finger. "One hand."

"That's the Breylu Dast that I know," Nellik said with a slithering grin. He pulled out the chair next to him.

Dast sat and slid the creaking chair forward. "Let's see what we have here," he said as he rested one arm atop the other.

Nellik patted his friend on the back and nodded. "I'm telling you," he grumbled. "They are using loaded dice."

"We'll see about that," Breylu said with a dismissive wave. His glowing green eyes shifted to a violet hue as they focused on the multicolored dice.

"Sir," the dealer yelled over the surrounding chatter. "Please, no cybernetic use at the table."

Dast's glowing gaze swiveled up, locking onto the young Islander Vandeni's face. Nellik crossed his arms. "I am simply making sure that you are not helping our opponents cheat," Breylu said, his brow lowering.

"For all I know, you're cheating," the dealer said with a shrug.

Nellik chuckled and removed his hat. A wave of silence circled their table and spread outward until the entire bar fell to hushed mutters and chiming glasses. A serpentine grin stretched across Nellik's face. "Poorly worded." The Draekalagon engulfed the dealer in an unblinking stare.

With a narrow scowl, Breylu's eyes shifted back to green. "Listen to me," he said, a tremble in his voice. "The owner of this fine establishment, Mister Corridan, I pay him good money to do—" He interrupted himself with a sigh. "Hmm, pretty much whatever I want here."

Nellik grunted. His head tilted sideways. "You do know Mister Corridan, don't you?"

The dealer stuttered. "Yes-yes, of course I do." His eyes moved back and forth between Breylu and Nellik as the gangsters reached below the table, each with a hand resting on their sidearm. The dealer's nervous swallow was the loudest noise in the saloon.

"Well I do too. Quite well," Dast said. Two other members of his gang began to inch toward the table, each prepared to draw arms. "And I know for damn sure, he'd be grateful if I put down a nervous little rookie dealer for givin' lip to one of his favorite customers."

Chatter circulated, growing loud and eager. Several patrons inched closer to the situation. Others stepped backward, more cautious than curious. The two bartenders stopped pouring drinks. Nellik surveyed the crowd, ready to fire upon onlookers who thought to intervene.

Breylu chuckled and thrust his gloved finger toward the dealer. "So why don't you deal the cards, call the hands and let us get back to having a good time? Or, if you still have an issue with me checking the dice…" His jaw tightened as he spoke through clenched teeth. The beaming green shine from his circular specs brightened, leaving a glow on his mask.

The dealer swallowed again. "Please place all buy-ins on the table." Sweat poured from his brow.

"Smart answer," Breylu said as he leaned back.

Nellik laughed and tossed his chips on the table. The bar resonated with a disappointed groan. Belligerent roars returned within moments, followed by the pentatonic melody of the electric harpsichord.

'At least have the decency to hire a good musician,' Nellik thought. 'This harpsichord player is a distraction to those in the room with a sense of rhythm.' The cards were coming out. He would have to block out the musical irritation. 'Oh, come on, Breylu. They're cheats. Just figure out how they're doing it.'

Breylu put in a hundred platinum, the table minimum. Nellik put in eight hundred. 'I can win it all back and then some on this hand.' Nellik's cards came. 'An excellent hand,' he thought. 'I have to win this one.'

"Any further bets?" the blue-skinned dealer shouted. The players remained still and silent. "Would anyone like to roll the dice for a double-down bet? Or will everyone be playing their hands?"

"I'll roll the dice," the player on the left side of the table said.

'No way,' Nellik thought. 'Not this time.'

The player rolled the dice, and the dealer flipped Nellik's cards. His thin reptilian lips widened with glee. Breylu looked upon the dice, his fingers on his chin. They rolled across the table, and one landed on orange. The other span on its corner. Nellik's fist tightened. His claws dug into his palm as the second die slowed, then stilled.

It too fell on orange.

'Double orange,' he thought. One of the only two rolls that could have bested his hand.

The dealer reached across the table and dragged Nellik's chips to the pile.

Nellik hissed. His eyes narrowed on Dast.

"I'm out," Breylu said. He tipped his hat and stood.

"No, Breylu. We can take these guys."

Breylu turned away.

Nellik stood and grabbed his shoulder. "C'mon, Breylu. I know they're cheating. I can catch them with you on the scene."

"Nellik." Breylu shook his head. "I scanned the dice. There were no abnormalities." He pointed toward the table. "What you got there are a couple of sharpshooters. And you don't play Wolf Jack against players with better dice skills than you."

"They are *not* better. They are cheating."

"Enough, Nellik." Dast's voice fell low and grim. "Just drop it. Tap out before you lose all your coin."

Nellik of Grathank's fangs slid over his lower lip. He eyed Breylu with spite. "You got it, boss," he said with a scraping snarl.

Nellik turned toward the table with a wide smile. "That's it for me, gentlemen." He extended his green hand to shake his opponents', both of whom returned the gesture. Nellik's narrow snout declined. "What are your names?"

"Clef," the man to the left said.

"Petrus," the other muttered.

"You may be sharp at shooting dice, but what about pistols?" Nellik whispered.

"Pardon?" Petrus asked.

"I still think the two of you are swindlers. And I want to challenge you to a duel. In the name of honor."

"What are the stakes?" Clef asked with a slow blink, shuffling a handful of chips.

"Double or nothing," Nellik said through a fang-filled grin. "Every coin you won from me during our match. We'll place the wager between us on the streets. Winner rides off with the pot."

"No thanks," Petrus said with an arrogant scoff. "I don't trust a temperamental lizard to keep his weapons set on incap. Especially one who can't stop grumbling about cheating, despite being unable to show any evidence."

Nellik's grin widened behind his flickering forked tongue. "Well, let's bury our mutual mistrust and play riverboat rules."

"A death match?" Clef asked with a sour look.

"Yes. Weapon power all the way up. Winner takes everything on the opponent's body, plus the wager."

The two Vandeni men looked to one another and laughed. The dealer kept his gaze aimed at the table.

Petrus sneered. "I don't trust your coin, lizard breath. You'll probably throw us silver instead of platinum."

Nellik fell back in his chair with a roar of laughter. "Your innocence and bigotry are amusing. But any child can tell the difference between platinum and silver." He looked toward the other gambler. "Take Clef here. Not by any means an attractive fellow. But I bet he knows how to identify all that platinum that he hasn't earned."

Petrus' hand fell to his beltline. Nellik smiled, reaching toward his own. Clef's arm smacked Petrus' chest. The two men scooted back as Nellik's hand surfaced from beneath the table. But he did not hold a weapon. Nellik held his data system. His clawed fingers tapped the screen, and he shoved the device their way.

"If you don't trust my coin," Nellik said, crossing his scaled green fingers, "trust my bounty."

Petrus leaned over Clef's shoulder. The blue glow of Nellik's data system rested on the gamblers' faces. "Six thousand platinum? You're wanted for six thousand platinum?"

Nellik nodded. "I trust that should cover the entirety of the wager. In fact, this doubles what I lost to the two of you."

"The Moon Shadow Riders, huh?" Clef asked, shuffling the chips in the palm of his hand.

"Don't think about collecting the bounty here." Nellik wagged his finger. "Ridgespire Marshal's Department is on our payroll. They'll kill you if you try to turn me in." He rested his elbow on the arm of the chair. His brown trench coat fell back, revealing the pistol strapped to his belt. "Unless you are afraid of a *temperamental lizard*."

"No, no," Clef said. "We'll do it, won't we, Petrus?"

"Sure," Petrus replied. "But we're both gunna be dueling. So, you better get yourself a partner."

Clef nodded. "One hour. A mile out from the southern entrance to the city outskirts. Where the lawmen won't arrest us."

"Good idea. If there's no witnesses, I can claim your deaths as self-defense." Nellik's words bled through his fangs. "I'll recruit a second partner." He turned around. "I look forward to serving the two of you justice."

"I'm sure you do, dragonrot," Petrus said with a mocking snicker.

'Don't shoot them here,' Nellik thought. 'Shoot them outside the city where you won't get arrested. They'll be just as dead. But no one will see.

No jail.' Nellik's anger was subdued by his thoughts. 'Not in the mood for a jailbreak.'

He moved across the card tables. Patrons scooted their chairs in, and drink servers rushed out of the way. Not uncommon reactions to a seven-foot-tall Draekalagon's gait. But Nellik took no offense. In fact, it amused him. A waitress steered far from his path. As his orange eyes pierced the slight Vandeni woman, her steps quickened. Nellik chuckled, peering through the smoke. A familiar shape leaned against the bar—the shape of Jarrus Thane, the fastest cannonslinger north of Vulture. Nellik's satisfaction grew. 'The Serpent's will guides this hunt.'

The pistoleer held a full drink in his shooting hand. Hopefully, he had not had too many. "Jarrus, my dear friend," Nellik said.

Jarrus glanced his way and offered an upward nod. "Nellik! How you feelin', partner?" His back and elbows slumped against the bar. "Enjoying the night off?"

"Yes, but I need your help."

Jarrus' slight smile refused to subside. "What can I do for ya, buddy?" He stared upon the crowd of patrons.

Nellik leaned into the outlaw's field of view. "I need your expertise in the field of weaponry to bring down a couple of gambling cheats."

Jarrus' eyes slanted toward him. "A duel?"

"Indeed."

Jarrus shook his head. "No can do, partner, I'm busy tonight."

Nellik stuttered. His clawed toes scuffed the surface of the rough wooden floor. "B-busy? You're just getting drunk."

"No, no." Jarrus' smile widened. "I'm doing recon."

"Recon?"

"Yeah." Jarrus leaned toward Nellik, whispering over the sharp notes of the harpsichord. "You see that girl in red? Over by the roulette table?"

The whisky on Jarrus' breath was stronger than the saloon's swirling scents of smoke, perfume and peculiar intoxicating mixes. Nellik's stomach churned as the cocktail of aromas invaded his heightened Draekalagon sense of smell. "Y-yes," he said.

"She and I, we're going to be spending the evening together."

Nellik's eyelids fluttered. "Jarrus," he said, clearing his throat. "That woman is an escort. All you need to spend the evening with her is a hundred platinum."

"Nellik, my reptilian friend. That is just the thing." His head fell low, and his eyes swiveled up. "I will pay with nothing but the pleasure of my company—worth more than a hundred platinum to any lady in need of a charming fellow."

Nellik squeezed between Jarrus and the nearby patron. "Come on, Jarrus. The lady in red can wait. Killing these sharpers can't."

"Killing?" He arched an eyebrow. "You challenged them to a riverboat match?"

"Indeed," Nellik said with a long grin. Surely, this would be the thrill that Jarrus needed to join him in this fight.

Jarrus sighed and chugged down the rest of his drink. "I'm sure one of the others will help ya out, partner. We're in the Moon Shadow Riders, after all." He pushed himself off the bar with his elbows. "Alright, I'm going in." He stood on the tips of his toes and unleashed a sharp pant in Nellik's face. "How's my breath?"

"Rancid."

Jarrus pulled a cigarillo from his vest pocket and placed it in his mouth. "I'll have to smoke some mouthwash, then." After pulling his belt up by the shining silver buckle, he stepped into the crowd. "Wish me luck, Nellik. I'll put in a good word for you with her friends. Maybe you can have yourself a pleasant evening if you're not dead later."

Nellik sighed, but the sound that came out resembled a growl. Surrounding patrons glanced his way, making their best effort to appear as though they were not doing so. The Draekalagon outlaw stomped forward with a heavy gait. "Where's Vinai?" he grumbled. The crowd cleared a path, much wider than he needed. "I will have to rely on a fellow Draekalagon to defend my honor."

His slit pupils widened. In the corner of the saloon, a figure sat in the shadows. Her pale golden eyes glinted behind the cloud of smoke arising from her pipe. His heavy steps moved toward the woman, who sat in solitude with her legs on the table. Her tail coiled the back of the chair and kept a firm embrace around her rifle.

"What do you want, Nellik of Grathank?" she asked.

He had yet to think of how to word the proposition for his fellow Shadow Rider. "Vinai of Oglund, I have a proposition for you." Well, that was a good place to start.

"Speak your mind," she said, removing the pipe from her mouth. "But do not waste my time."

'Waste your time?' Nellik thought. 'You're just sitting here.'

He stood tall and removed his hat. "I offer you the chance to defend our honor. Our honor as children of the Draelek Empire. The honor of our clans, both of Draelek birth, and our Moon Shadow brethren. In honor of the will of the Infinite Serpent—"

"The Infinite Serpent?" Vinai's snout flared. The pipe clicked between her fangs, hanging from the side of her mouth. "Do you suppose that the Infinite's Serpent wills one of its children to partake in a death duel over a card game?"

"How did you know about that already?"

Smoke streamed from her long snout. "That's why I'm sitting at this table. I can see and hear everything in this creaky saloon." She motioned to the crowd of belligerent patrons.

Nellik made a tight fist. His claws dug into his palm. "The Infinite Serpent will bless this hunt. The Infinite Serpent offers no favor for deception."

Vinai's chin rose. "The Infinite Serpent sees no honor in the pursuit of a personal vendetta. Surely you remember the creeds of the ancient runes."

Nellik placed his hat back on his head and looked away. "The Infinite Serpent and I have our... own arrangement."

Vinai nodded, her blue tail stroking the stock of her rifle. "Well, I hope the Serpent's eternal grace blesses your path on this evening, Nellik of Grathank. I, on the other hand, will continue to follow the path of the runes."

"Path of the runes..." Nellik scoffed and pretended to hold in a chuckle. "I must have missed the *rune of the outlaw sharpshooter*."

"Remember the hymn of the 'Thraeliss Rune.' 'Protect those with whom you share kinship and clan.' As you say, the Shadow Riders are our clan now."

Nellik turned away. He spoke out the side of his mouth, leaving the female Draekalagon's company. "Well, you're not offering much protection, Vinai."

"Nor are you," Vinai said with a soft hiss. "You can't even protect yourself."

'Forget her,' Nellik thought. In the crowd, Nellik saw Lynara Sikora. She moved among the patrons with a frantic pace and a suspicious glare.

Nellik cut through the crowd. "Lynara!" he yelled.

She turned and stared for a long moment. But she carried on without speaking.

"Don't pretend you don't notice me, Lynara." Nellik bared his fangs.

"Nellik, can't talk now," Lynara's speedy voice said, somehow coming from behind. "Very busy. Making bombs."

Nellik spun toward her. His tail almost knocked over an elderly patron. "Apologies," he said with a tip of his hat. As the old lady collected herself, Lynara inched away. "Lynara, wait." His long arm grabbed hold of the woman's blue jacket.

She stomped her boot on the floor. "What, Nellik?" Her feathery hair, dyed jet black, fell over her face. "Already told you. Quite busy. And you are drawing attention to me." With a crinkle of her small pointy nose, her tone changed from angry to animated. "Trying to blend in. Be another face in the crowd. Everyone notices you, Nellik. You're large and quite menacing."

"Well, you're blending in well if you can sneak up on me."

"Thank you! Been practicing." Her eyes swiveled back and forth. "I'm stealing material for bombs. Anything useful to add to my arsenal. Surprising what people don't notice that you take from them." She shook the pouch attached to her thigh. Its metal contents clattered together.

"Why are you making bombs?" Nellik whispered, eying the pouch. "We don't have a job tomorrow."

The music stopped. "*Always* on the job, Nellik." Intent nods accompanied her words. "*Always* gotta be prepared. *Always* stayin' sharp." Her words carried farther with no music to muddle them, but Lynara paid no mind. "What if we were to get arrested tonight, Nellik? What would you say then, hmm? Probably be pretty happy that Lynara has some makeshift explosives on her, hmm?" Nellik tried to interject to quiet her down, but he could not get a word in. "Explosions are the key to escape. Bombs make explosions. That's why I make bombs, Nellik."

Nellik looked around and let out a nervous laugh, trying to play off Lynara's rant as a joke. Nearby patrons eyed the outlaws for a moment before returning to their conversations and drinks.

"Listen." He spoke with a harsh whisper. "This is a job," he said. "Test those explosives on some live subjects with me." The harpsichord tapered into another upbeat tune.

"Hmm." Lynara scratched her chin. "Tempting... but... no!" Her finger lifted. "Too much distraction. Must stay on task."

"Lynara, come on!"

But the demolitionist withdrew and blended among the crowd.

"Athenis be damned," Nellik said, stomping away. He whispered to himself, "Why am I surprised? I ride with outlaws. Selfish by nature *and* nurture."

A group sitting at a table looked at him with confused disgust. Nellik's eyes of fire burned into a Vandeni man with a cyber-monocle, which fell off his face when he scooted his chair back. Nellik stuck his tongue out, hissing at the man. The entire group of patrons recoiled.

Nellik let out a snarling laugh as he passed by them. 'Where is he?' After circling the bar a few times, his eyes rolled. How tired he had grown of looking for members of his gang. "Giavi!" His harsh voice shook the saloon's flimsy tables. The crowd quieted, and the music slowed. Folks turned to the outlaw. He crossed his arms, and his long tail tightened. 'Damn it, where is he?'

"Umm, sir?" a voice said from behind.

With a vicious snarl, Nellik turned to see a man in a ruby-red suit standing behind him. "I am in *no* mood."

"I understand," he said, raising his white gloves. "But can you please keep your voice down? Maybe sit down and try to enjoy your evening? You're disturbing the other customers."

Nellik showed his fangs. "Oh, am I now? And why should I care about that?"

"Well, sir." He smacked his lips together. "You're drawing a lot of attention. And considering that a lot of our operations aren't entirely legal—"

"Neither is tying you to the trunk of an indigo cactus." Nellik's shadow shrouded the well-dressed man. He swallowed and took a step back. "But I won't let that stop me." With a wide grin, he walked by the man, grunting, "You have a pleasant evening. Giavi!" he shouted again. A bit quieter this time.

"What is it, Nellik?!" Giavi's high-pitched voice called out. He held on to his fedora, squeezing through the crowd. "Do you need medical?"

"No, my young friend," Nellik said with open arms. "Today, I need the combat side of your 'combat medic' profession."

"Wha-what do you mean?"

Nellik chuckled. "You and I, we have a duel with a couple of sharpshooters. Lots of money to be had."

Giavi's brown eyes widened. Sweat trailed down his deep blue skin. "Wait, Nellik. I've never been in a duel before."

"It's easy," Nellik said. He reached for his belt and pulled his pistol from its holster. "Just pull the trigger and they are dead." He flipped the weapon and extended it toward Giavi. "Come on, my friend. I need you on this."

"Umm, I don't know." Giavi's hand shook. His bitten fingernails clenched the pistol's white grip.

"It'll be fine," he said through a shaking smile. "Trust me."

"No!" Breylu stepped between Nellik and Giavi, slapping his hand over the pistol. "Keep him out of this."

"Boss, come on," Nellik said, looking skyward. "I'm out of options here."

"No, you're not." Breylu shoved the pistol into Nellik's chest. "Hire a cannonslinger. They're all over Ridgespire."

"I... can't afford that."

"Of course you can't." Breylu's head turned toward Giavi. "But that doesn't mean you involve him. He's just a kid. And he has nothing to do with your dead-end justice."

"This is a gang!" Nellik said, lifting his chin. "We are supposed to cover each other."

Dast leaned forward. His voice fell into deep static. "We are. So why don't you stop asking the rest of the gang to lay their lives down for you and *you* alone? No one should have to die for your stupidity."

"No one *has* to," Nellik said, a bloodthirsty bite behind his words. "I'm only offering."

Breylu's disdain seeped through his mask and circular eye coverings. "Giavi, find a spot at a table. I'll meet you there."

"Sure thing, boss," Giavi said with a nod before making his exit.

Breylu sighed and took a slow step toward Nellik.

The Dreakalagon's feet stuck to the grimy floor as he stepped back. "Say, boss, what do you say you back me up—"

"No."

Nellik's fiery eyes tightened. "You don't even know what I was going to say."

"I do." Breylu's voice croaked over the upbeat music and the boisterous crowd. "You want me to aid in your reckless endeavor."

Nellik leaned closer. "It's not reckless. It's the founding members of the Shadow Riders in a duel. We can't lose!"

Breylu shook his head. "You are on your own."

"Come on," Nellik said. "Help me take out a couple of swindlers. Where's your sense of adventure?"

"You know what is damning to any sense of adventure, Nellik?" His voice fell low, and a metallic hiss accompanied his words. "Shock-cannon fire. It'll melt your skin, cauterize your organs, and stop your heart." He stood tall, and his heavy cybernetic leg stomped the wooden floor. "I'm not dying because you are sour that you lost in cards."

Dast stepped away. Nellik followed, reaching for his shoulder. "Boss, think about it. It's a good deal for us. I could pay you back the coin I owe you out of our winnings!"

Breylu shrugged off Nellik's scaled hand. His spine coiled forward like a rising serpent. "*Now* you care to pay your debts? Unbelievable. You'll have to live with the consequences of your actions. Or die with them."

"I've asked everyone," Nellik said. "Help me out, boss. Just one more time. One more duel to end my debts."

Breylu's glowing green eyes shifted to a soft blue. "No. But if you don't survive, I'll make sure that's what they put on your headstone." His hand elevated. "Nellik of Grathank: A Life and Death of Duels and Debts." With a mocking, grim laugh, Breylu trudged off.

"Good to know who has my back in times of peril." Nellik crossed his arms and stood aslant.

"If it's a dueling partner you're looking for," a soft, approaching voice said, "Perhaps I could be of aid."

Crow. He had not even thought to ask Crow. "*You* want to help *me*?"

Her black lipstick was smeared on the tip of her thin white cigarillo. "That's what you are seeking, is it not? Someone to accompany you in battle? To abet in the neutralization of some ravenous card cheats?"

Her Imperial accent—so proper. Her etiquette—so polite. So irksome. "You—" Nellik shook his head. "You've only been riding with us for three months. And you're a tech specialist. Do you even know how to fire a shock-cannon?"

"I received basic training in the Imperium." She placed a hand on her hip. Her pale blue eyes shined with her soft smile. "And I have been receiving occasional lessons from Vinai."

Like most of her fellow Imperial countrywomen, Crow was quite tall. Eye contact required only a slight downward adjustment of Nellik's gaze. "Lessons from Vinai," he said with a scoff. "How old are you, anyway?"

"Twenty-two." With a slow nod, her eyes hid behind her hat. The brim cast a shadow over her grey face.

Nellik bowed his head. "Twenty-two... And the boss gave me a lecture for inviting Giavi along. Because *he* was too young."

"Well you're not inviting me, Nellik." Standing tall, she pushed her black trench coat to the side. "I'm inviting myself," she said with a long drag of her white cigarillo.

"How typical is my luck?" Nellik locked his thumbs in his brown leather belt. "I ride in a gang with the most feared outlaw in Vanda, the fastest pistol in the northern desert, the best sniper that Clan Oglund has bred in a hundred years, the most skilled demolitionist in the criminal underworld, a multitalented combat medic from Rogue Haven... and the only one that offers to aid me in a duel is an Imperial cyber-technician." He growled through his snout. "Perhaps Vinai is right. My ways have angered the Infinite Serpent."

"Well, I am happy to help you earn the Serpent's favor back."

Nellik chuckled, more amused by the remark than he wished to let on. "Have you ever even been in a duel?"

"No, I have not." Crow reached into her coat pocket for her ocular visor. She placed the glass device over her eyes. "But I pick up on things quickly." The visor beeped and brightened with neon shades of pink, violet and cyan. "You saw me at the Cold Brook job."

"Cracking a safe is a bit different from firing a shock-cannon in a fight to the death." Nellik's eyes rolled to the crossing ceiling beams. "Perhaps this is what I deserve. To die side by side with an Imperial. Just what will they say about me when my body returns to Grathank? Will they even offer me a proper burial?"

With a fake smile, his hand fell to his holstered sidearm. "Has this been your plan all along? To help kill a poor Draekalagon so you have stories to tell your Imperial friends? Maybe create some anti-Draelek propaganda?"

Crow's blue eyes widened with intensity. Her thin lips fell to a slight frown. "I have as much loyalty to the High Imperium as I do to Draelekar: none."

Nellik's clawed finger pointed upward. "Well, at least we have one thing in common."

"That we do, Nellik."

Nellik grunted. "Well. Seeing that you are full of unsubstantiated confidence..." He adjusted his hat and pulled up his coat by the lapels. "Let's go get shot to death in the middle of the desert." His toes scraped the wooden floor with his steps. "At the very least, we can laugh from the grave when the gang has to replace us."

"I agree," Crow said, following behind.

"If we win, I'll drop the platinum I owe Breylu on his lap later tonight—along with the heads of my opponents. That'll show him."

"That's… probably exactly what he wants, Nellik. Sans the severed heads."

"True."

After gathering their weapons, Crow and Nellik stepped under the amethyst-and-sapphire night sky of Eramaa. Nellik pulled his coat around his neck as the desert air cooled his blood. Many of the towns-people in Ridgespire turned their heads at what must have been a pecu-liar sight: an Imperial woman and a Draekalagon man, riding side by side on truganback.

The starlight guided their path to the outskirts of town. The trugans' claws crunched the sand and gravel. Indigo cacti bathed in the clouded white beams of twin moonlight. Nellik looked to the sparkling heavens and took a deep breath.

Two figures stood in shadow. Their smug faces became clear as Nellik and Crow approached.

"I see you have a partner," Petrus said, hands over his belt buckle. "Unexpected. A lizard and a greyskin drawing cannons together. Now I've seen everything."

Clef chuckled, cleaning the scope on his pistol. "You must have been truly desperate."

"She rides with me, card cheats." Nellik's feet stomped the dirt as he stepped out of his saddle. "She's a feared outlaw."

"You hear that, Pertrus?" Clef asked, leaning toward his dueling part-ner. "We get another bounty to collect."

"Speaking of which," Nellik said with an extension of his arm. "Your side of the wager: lay out your coin."

Pertrus reached inside the pannier on his trugan's back. He slung a sack of coins at Nellik's feet.

Nellik reached for the sack. "Watch my back," he whispered to Crow. He eyed the two gamblers. "Gotta make sure that these coins aren't made of *silver*." He shook the bag before pulling it open. His fingers shuffled through the coins. "Wait a minute, there is only fifteen hundred platinum in here. I lost at least two thousand to your slight hands."

"Take it easy, lizard." Clef stepped over to his trugan and tugged on a second sack to the sound of clinking coins. "The rest is right here. You can take it off our bodies once we're dead." He cackled on his own words.

"Laugh while you can." Nellik caressed the handle of his holstered pistol with the tip of his claw. "You won't be laughing in a few minutes."

Clef and Petrus drew their weapons. Nellik drew his. "Crow, prepare to fire," he whispered. Nellik squinted and looked behind. "Crow, draw your weapon!"

The Imperial woman's attention was on her data system. She tapped on the screen with swift aggression. "Please wait a moment," she said with a surly tone.

"How can you possibly be sending a message right now?" Nellik asked, stomping the dirt.

Clef and Petrus laughed. "Should we just shoot them now?" Petrus asked.

"Don't you dare," Nellik said, taking aim.

"Whoa, whoa." Clef raised his weapon in turn. "Let's do this with a sense of tradition. Twenty paces back. All weapons drawn simultaneously."

Petrus raised his shock-cannon as well. "I'd hate to kill this poor Imperial lady that you somehow manipulated into coming out here." He spit as his finger twitched over the trigger of his pistol. "At least not before she is armed with more than a data system."

"The data system is recording you," Crow said, lips pursed. "I'm feeding a direct recording to the rest of our gang. If they find out that you killed us without proper dueling terms, they will give you a far slower death than those pistols are about to give us."

'What is she doing?' Nellik thought. 'More importantly, what am *I* doing?'

"I don't believe you," Clef said with a tilt of his head.

Crow's eyebrows lifted. Her gaze remained on her data system. "Shoot us then. I'll pray you meet some semblance of mercy."

Nellik took a steady step forward. "Or we do this like gentlemen." He gestured toward Crow. "And like a... lady."

"Hmm?" Crow's loud screen-tapping stopped. She looked up. "Oh, thank you!"

"Okay," Clef said. "On a count of three, we holster our weapons."

Nellik nodded.

"One—two—three."

The three men relaxed their aim, though Petrus' arm was the slowest to come down.

Clef's boot tapped against the dirt. "So, if everyone is ready, we can begin this duel."

Nellik's eyes slanted to his fellow Moon Shadow Rider. "Crow?"

"Just a minute—and done." Crow looked up with a grin. "Okay, twenty paces back. Did I hear that correctly?"

"Yes," said Clef. "Pick your weapon."

"I shall," Crow said. "And one more question. Optical aiming support is allowed, yes?" She pointed to the neon glow of her optical visor.

"I'm using it," said Petrus. "It's dark out here."

"Indeed," Crow said with a nod. She unstrapped a rifle from her trugan's pannier. With a groan, she pulled the weapon over her chest, checking the chamber.

"A sniper rifle?" Nellik whispered while both opponents had their backs turned. "You do realize that they are using pistols? They'll have fired before you can reach for it."

Crow hunched over and strapped the rifle to her back. "I would rather sacrifice speed for accuracy." The shock-cannon strained the Imperial woman's posture, too long and heavy for her slender frame. "And it is the weapon with which I am most familiar."

Why bother trying to convince Crow of anything? Death's trail was paved toward Nellik of Grathank. The fight against fate was futile. He pulled his scatter cannon from his trugan's pannier. Maybe he could take the swindlers down with him. One well-placed blast from a scatter cannon was all it would take.

Nellik lined up, facing Petrus. Crow stood next to him, facing Clef. The wind passed between the opponents with a sharp whisper.

"Twenty paces—begin," Clef said.

The rival pairs stepped back, facing one another.

"Hey, Crow," Nellik mumbled.

"Yes, Nellik?" Crow asked with a peculiar tone of merriment.

"I just wanted to say—regardless of what happens, thanks for having my back out here."

She looked away, hiding the slight blush in her grey cheeks. "It's my pleasure, Nellik."

"Stop!" Clef yelled. All duelists planted their feet in the dirt. "I'm gunna count down from three. We pull cannons on 'draw.'"

Petrus' hand twitched over his holster.

"It's not too late to back out," Clef added. "No one *has* to die here."

"What do you think?" Nellik spoke out of the side of his mouth. "Should we take that escape route?"

Crow shrugged. "It is entirely up to you."

Nellik hunched forward. He kicked his foot into the gravel like a bull preparing to charge. "We ain't asking for your mercy, dice loaders." He turned to the side. "So, unless you are asking for it, begin your countdown!"

"Okay," Clef said. "Your lives are yours to throw away." He clutched the handle of his pistol. "Three…"

Crow's hand hovered over her optical system. Nellik reached for the scatter cannon strapped to his leg.

"Two…"

"Crow," Nellik muttered. "Set that aiming system already. Get a hand on your rifle."

But Crow's hand remained on the visor.

"One…"

"Crow!" Nellik hissed.

Her finger slid over a button on the device. "Focus on shooting, Nellik."

"Draw!"

Nellik's long hand drew his heavy scatter cannon with the speed of a striking scorpion. He took aim, but the opposing duelists did not. They screamed, grasping their foreheads in distress.

Crow reached behind and raised the sniper rifle. Nellik fired a blast from his scatter cannon. A web of bright electricity launched from the barrel, striking Petrus and Clef. A second volley of shots came from Crow. Two sniper blasts streamed through the air and struck both of their convulsing bodies.

Echoes of thunder roared by, following the cannon fire. The four trugan roared and squealed.

Nellik's long jaw fell, gaping. "How did…?" He choked on his words. "What did…?" He took off his hat and scratched the top of his rough head. "Did you hack their optical systems?"

Crow let her rifle hang forward, keeping the stock against her breast. "I did." Her face remained blank, and her chin tucked in. "Little flash of light in their eyes."

Nellik's head tilted and his eyes narrowed. "How?"

"Quite simple, really." Crow turned toward him and leaned forward. "Their targeting systems were secured by only a basic encryption. I locked onto the signal which connects their weapons to their optical devices." She pointed toward her own colorful two-eyed optical system. "I cracked the code and connected their targeting systems to mine."

"So, you blinded them." Nellik took a step forward. His orange eyes narrowed in a squint.

"Of course, I did." Her brow rose. She walked toward the motionless Clef and Petrus. "You were certain that they were cheats. Did you really expect me to take a chance on them playing fairly in a death duel?"

Nellik followed the tall woman. "I cannot argue against that logic."

"Better to cheat than die."

"Agreed."

They approached the smoking corpses of the two gamblers. Crow leaned over Clef. Nellik rolled Petrus over on his back. "Let's see what they got," he said.

He searched Petrus' pockets. A few more loose coins and a pocket watch. But nothing much else of value. "Tell me something," he said.

"Hmm?" Crow mumbled. Her optical system hummed and beeped, scanning Clef's corpse.

"Did you really have a feed going to the gang?"

"Of course not." Crow looked up. "They just seemed childish enough to believe it."

Nellik chuckled. He turned to the deceased gamblers' trugan. They stood back-to-back, their tails tucked between their legs. "I wonder what's on their trugan. I'll set my cannon to incap just in case."

"You should be fine," Crow said, patting down Clef's body. "They've shown no signs of hostility. Something tells me that these two didn't treat them very well."

"More of a reason to be glad for their deaths," Nellik said. He sidled toward the trugan that held the second coin sack.

"Certainly." Crow began to cycle through Clef's data system.

The mounted reptilian beasts backed off, extending their forked tongues. The trugan with the coin sack let out a growling hiss.

However, Nellik whispered some soothing words in Draelek. The beast eased and allowed him to reach for the sack. He shuffled his hands through the coins and let out a coarse laugh. "There's only a hundred platinum in here."

Crow turned around. "Not all that surprising."

"Yes," Nellik said, shaking the sack. "A bunch of five-platinum coins. Gave it a nice sound effect."

Crow peeked his way. "So that leaves you with sixteen hundred platinum. Hardly enough to pay back Mister Dast."

"Well, you're taking half the money," Nellik said, tossing the bag of coins next to the other.

Crow shook her head. "No need. The duel was yours. The wager is yours."

"I have a plan," Nellik said with a smile. "We can sell the weapons, their clothes and the trugan. I could actually make a decent coin off these ugly corpses. At least let me give you something."

Crow chuckled. "I meant what I said. Repayment is not necessary. I found the experience quite exhilarating; that is reward enough."

Nellik stood over her. "Well, please do tell me if *you* ever need anyone killed."

Crow nodded with a long blink. "I'll make sure that I do." She scrolled through the data system and paused on a page filled with notes and diagrams of dice. "Oh my. Nellik, look at this."

"What is it?" Nellik squatted, peeking over her shoulder.

"They weren't using loaded dice." She pointed to the screen. "But they did know that those dice were biased in favor of orange and blue."

"How?"

"They did weeks of research, discreetly watching those tables." She showed him a diagram. "They found pairs of dice that were in circulation at the saloon and digitally marked them with their optical system. Even if the dealers moved the dice to different tables, our friends could find them again." Crow shrugged. "Is it truly cheating to discover a bias in the laws of probability?"

Nellik stood and crossed his arms. With a serpentine grin and a brash grunt, he looked to Crow. "Any chance you wanna go play that table? Place some bets on orange and blue?"

She returned a coy smile. "Nothing would please me more."

Author's Note

Good tidings, adventurers! I hope that you have enjoyed your time in Vanda, the High Imperium and on the sea. Now that the dust has settled, let us gather by the fire, sharing drink and company. These tales were a pleasure to write, and I am honored that you allowed me to share them with you. If you find the time, please leave an honest review on Amazon, Goodreads, Bookbub and/or anywhere else that you share your love of reading. Reviews are what help bring readers into the world of Endless Frontier and we could always use more companions on this journey!

These tales were written to stand on their own as an entry point into this series, while also providing supplementary material for Vanden veterans. If this was your first trail blazed across this strange realm and you find yourself wanting more, make sure you read the full-length *Endless Frontier: The Hunter and the Knight* following Kasta Krane, now a treasure hunter, on a quest for a mystical blade. If you crave *even more* cannon-slinging, trugan chases and snarky anti-heroes, be sure to sign up for my mailing list at brettlurie.com/newsletter to receive a free novella featuring Nellik of Grathank and the rest of the Moon Shadow Riders executing a daring heist. You heard Crow reference her capability on The Cold Brook Job – see for yourself in the aptly named *The Cold Brook Job: An Endless Frontier Folktale.*

Many more fables of companionship, heroism and ancient magics await. When Athenis rises again, a new epic adventure dawns. What will become of Vanda when The High Imperium occupies her lands, in search of militant terrorists? Find out in *Endless Frontier: Blood and Soul,* coming to your kindles and shelves in 2025.

ABOUT THE AUTHOR

Brett grew up splitting his adventure appetite between fantasy quests through Tolkien's vistas and Eastwood standoffs in Sergio Leone westerns. His debut weird western saga, *Endless Frontier* pulses with reverence for flawed protagonists, supernatural showdowns, and mystical science magic. A scholar of political theory during his academic studies, Brett chose to apply his knowledge of statecraft to his woldbuilding.

An avid RPG gamer and comic book collector, Brett brings captivating women leads, amphibious races, and a magic system based on wireless electricity powered by charge crystals. With an endless frontier to explore, Brett looks to expand tales of high-voltage rivalry and unlikely alliances. His happy place is in the mountains with a cup of coffee on the table and his cat, Raven, on his lap.

www.ingramcontent.com/pod-product-compliance
Lightning Source LLC
Chambersburg PA
CBHW061523310726
48972CB00008B/2311